NODDING

Jacqueline Druga

Nodding
By Jacqueline Druga

Covert Art by Elliott Chan

With gratitude beyond reason, I wish to thank: Cindy P, Rita, Bonnie, Sonia and Jhanelle.

ABOUT THE AUTHOR
Jacqueline Druga is a native of Pittsburgh, Pa. She is a prolific writer and filmmaker. Her published works include genres of all types, but favors post-apocalypse and apocalypse writing.

A single mother of four, Jacqueline is also a musician. She resides in a small town outside of Pittsburgh with her family. Of all her accomplishments, Jacqueline is most proud of being a grandmother. Her grandchildren reside with her and are the light of her life.

Jacqueline welcomes emails. You can reach her at greatoneas@gmail.com

Dedication

This story is dedicated to all the brave parents who must make difficult choices for the sake of their children.

District 3

August 2 – Year 10 P.D. (Post-Detaining)

Streaks of pink moved across the grey early morning sky, and she took that as a good sign. The sun would come out, even for just a little, but it would have to struggle to power its way through the dust and debris that remained in the atmosphere.

The sun would eventually win. Life goes on. Things would grow again all over, not just in protected areas.

She stood before the huge stone wall; she remembered when it was erected and how it took only a short time to make it. It was an entrance to one of five cities deemed cut off from civilization.

District 3.

At one time, she lived over a hundred miles from District 3 but the Detaining caused her to move closer. Perhaps that was what saved her life when the Six Day War broke out.

Six days was all it took.

A war brought on by anger, agony, and rage.

Man against man in frustration over no one's ability to do anything.

Why live? Why care?

She did, because a part of her knew.

That was what drove her to the wall faithfully for ten years, a deep gut-wrenching feeling.

One day … maybe.

At first, when she could breathe again and think clearly, her heart still aching, she took what money she could and bought a trailer. Everything was cheaper then. People just wanted to sell things because they didn't care. She packed it up with supplies and moved twenty miles outside of District 3. That was as close as she could get. A military blockade kept her from getting close.

Back then, she was far from the only one. Thousands made the pilgrimage to District 3 and she supposed the same occurred at the other four Districts, as well.

She, like the others, gave up her old life in a vain attempt at hope.

She gave up everything after the Detaining and moved her ambitions to the District. She was waiting.

She was grateful that her focus was District 3. Of them all, it was the easiest to get close to after the military blockade was removed.

That took three months and a lot of construction noise.

When they rolled out, she saw how sealed in the District was, and what great lengths they'd taken to do so.

District 3 was in a city that formed a triangle and nestled in the V of two merging rivers.

All access bridges were destroyed and along the riverbed, high electrical fences had been erected.

Therefore, the determined pilgrimage trucked 48 miles north to cross the eastern river then travel back toward District 3.

The long side of the tri-sided city was protected by a two-mile thick concrete wall, twenty feet high with electrical wire on top and a steel door that couldn't be touched.

She learned that fact when a man decided to pound on the door and scream, 'let us in'. His fist barely touched it before he was electrocuted.

The wall was the only structure that stood for miles. Buildings, homes, and everything else was flattened, sending a clear-cut message, "nothing shall live here or near here". Nevertheless, that didn't stop the pilgrimage.

They moved into the debris-filled area, setting up like refugees in a tent city.

During the first year, many more showed up, and everyone worked together with the same purpose.

Waiting. Hoping. Listening.

And during the night, when all was quiet and they sat by their small fires, they could hear the cries flowing out from the District, cries of sadness and pain, cries of loss, echoing through the night air.

With each cry she heard, her heart ached. She closed her eyes and thought, *Was that her? I'm here. Oh, God, Baby, I'm right here.*

It was the torturous music of the night, every night for a year.

Then it grew silent.

Still they waited.

Family never lost track of or hope for her. They sent her what she needed and visited often.

Every day when the morning broke, without fail, she would walk to the wall, place a slash mark there, then turn to the steel door and toss something at it.

She kept track of the days and tested the electrical current.

Every day it remained on.

She tried many times over the years. She and others would plot their break-in like criminals in the night, only to be thwarted by the authorities or other elements.

She was never arrested, only occasionally detained. She always returned to her camp and told the people, "One day, it'll be safe enough to open the gate." One day.

She vowed she'd be there when that happened.

For two years, the group remained diligent.

Then they started to leave, lose hope, give up.

She didn't.

She stayed.

It had gotten to the point where there wasn't any communication. No television, no radio.

By the fifth year, only the strong remained, and the thousands had dwindled to hundreds.

She and the others were not even aware there was a war in the sixth year until a man showed up hoping that the war caused an end to the madness, that perhaps District 3 was open.

It wasn't.

Cities had been destroyed, civilization scattered, new governments had formed, yet, despite all that, the gates remained charged.

Someone somewhere controlled that.

She stopped hearing from her family after the news of the war. She felt in her soul that they were lost to the tragic events.

It wasn't long after the war when the sky darkened and the temperatures dropped, and everyone started to leave.

They all left.

Only she remained.

New foliage had grown and died while she was there. She survived easily. Years earlier, pilgrims had tapped into an old water line, creating a well of sorts. It flowed with water as if those in charge of District 3 kept it going on purpose. Nevertheless, she didn't trust it would always flow, so every day she filled containers. When the others left and abandoned their belongings, she kept them all and filled their containers with water, restocked their food.

A man named Madison built a small greenhouse in year two. It grew plentiful crops, so much so that when the number of pilgrims was few, they dehydrated what they could over an open fire.

But when the sky turned perpetually grey, the growth in the greenhouse died.

She didn't worry. She had enough food.

When she needed meat, she didn't have to go far. Deer were easy to trap and kill. There were so many.

For two years, she was completely alone, but that didn't stop her from checking the gate daily. Nor did it stop her from calling out 'Hello!' every night and listening for some sort of response.

Usually she'd hear something, and that made her stay. It gave her more reason.

Time moved on until the day the markings on the concrete wall told her it was ten years and three weeks since she had arrived.

It was warmer that day, and the sky was clearing. She knew something was up when she went to the well and it was dry.

The water, for the first time in years, stopped running.

She walked to the wall, and with a stone, made a slash mark. Then she grabbed a portion of leftover rabbit and, as she did every day, tossed it at the door.

Nothing.

Nothing. Not a sound or a sizzle, just a thump.

She lifted the meat again, stepped back, and tossed it at the door.

Again … nothing.

Her heart beat strongly, her breathing labored, and her eyes widened.

She raced back to her little camp not ten feet away, grabbed her 'piercing stick' which she used on animals and headed back to the door.

With slight apprehension, she extended the stick and pressed on the now-rusted door.

Not only was there no electrical repercussion but something else occurred.

For the first time in ten years … the door opened.

She walked in.

PART ONE: RELEASE

Chapter One

TEN YEARS EARLIER – August 24

Heathrow Airport – London: Patient Zero

Ren Turner was little enough to dart in and out of people standing at the gate to retrieve his ball. At six years old he was old enough to annoy people and his mother knew it. Shelly Turner was already at her wits' end. She just wanted to get back to her home in Virginia. That, she knew, was a long way off.

Her husband had left with the other children, the older ones, three days earlier. Shelly stayed behind with Ren, who had a fever, sniffles, and a diagnosis of the common flu, which kept them in London longer. Ren felt better; he exhibited that as he raced around chasing his ball.

They called their flight number and the passengers boarded. Shelly called his name with a scold, "Ren, now." He hurried to his mother's side.

The man in front of her just smiled when Ren bumped into his legs.

"I am so sorry," Shelly told him. "He is just wired."

"That's fine, I have two boys of my own," he said. "All grown now. Although back in the day, a little dose of cold medicine did the trick on flights."

Shelly winced. "I think that's the problem. I gave him some. It did the opposite."

The man smiled. "Ah, hyper first. He'll crash on the plane." He winked. "Bet me."

"Let's hope." Shelly chuckled. "It's a long flight."

They boarded. Ren argued with his mother that he wanted to sit in the aisle seat. Shelly agreed reluctantly then realized it probably was the best thing. At least he wouldn't bother the person by the window. Sitting three across would make for a long flight, but it was the first flight back to the States that they could get.

Ren remained restless until they allowed electronics to be used, and then he was consumed with his game.

Shelly made small talk with the woman next to her, telling her story of how the family had to return home at different times. It was the first time Shelly informed the woman that the entire family was able to go on a story with her husband. He was a journalist with a huge news organization. They hadn't been home in months, but the children did get to see three continents and eight countries.

The conversation passed some time. It was when the woman next to her to said, "I think that cold medicine is finally kicking in," that Shelly glanced at Ren.

His eyes fluttered and his head nodded.

She smiled. "You're tired now, baby. Here …" She reached around him. "Let me put back your seat."

Just as she reached to do so, Ren's eyes popped open wide.

"Ren?" she questioned.

He hissed—long and loudly. Ren hissed again, shot a glare to Shelly, and before she could register what was occurring, he jumped from his seat.

Fast, like a scurrying cat, he raced over the tops of the seats and the heads of the passengers and flung his body at the flight attendant who stood at the front of the aisle.

The weight of his small body with the raging momentum knocked the flight attendant off balance, and they both fell to the floor.

With an angry growl and rapid blurred movements, Ren's hands whipped about. His hands clawed into the flight attendant repeatedly, shredding her skin, ripping her apart as if he were digging for a buried treasure all while his mouth bit, pulled, then spat her flesh.

14

She screamed in horror, blooding pouring from every wound.

Shelly had lunged forward when Ren first took off, but her attempts to grab him were futile, and lifting him from the flight attendant was impossible.

She cried out his name hysterically, pleading him to stop, calling for help.

It took four male passengers and an air marshal to seize Ren. However, the five of them couldn't control him and they eventually had to restrain him.

Even restrained, Ren struggled and thrashed like a rabid animal and did so the entire return trip, which had been diverted, back to London.

He was out of control, didn't respond to Shelly at all, nor to any attempts to calm him.

What had happened to her son? Shelly was at a loss and buried in a world of confusion and pain. There was nothing she could do but watch her child and sob from the bottom of her heart.

Chapter Two

New York City, NY

"This is Tom," that was how Tom Gibson answered the phone. No need for professionalism or to answer the phone, 'World News Network' or even pleasantries, it was his work cell and very few people called it.

He rubbed his eyes, he was tired and his day was just beginning. Getting a phone call at five a.m. wasn't a normal occurrence and he knew it had to come from overseas.

He paused before entering the production booth to take the call.

"Got a plane diverting back to Heathrow. My guy here says a passenger went nuts and attacked the stewardess."

"Probably drugs or something like the last time. Let me—"

"Tom, they're quarantining the plane."

Tom paused. "Really. Then there's obviously more. Stay on it. See if you can get me age, info and so forth on the passenger. Let's get a jump on this first. Get what you can and I'll connect with the affiliate this half-hour news."

He ended the call and entered the booth. "We're gonna make a spot for some breaking news in London. Find me time," Tom dictated, then turned to a production assistant. "Get in touch with the Ministry of Health in the UK; see if they have some sort of virus alert that would cause an immediate quarantine of a plane."

The production assistant nodded.

"Then hit the usual, CDC, WHO," he rattled, and stared at the monitor and to the news anchorwoman. "She looks tired. Get make up on her at commercial."

The tech to his right said, "You look tired, too."

16

Tom fluttered his lips. "I'm always tired."

And he was. He worked long hours, starting his day at five a.m. As the executive producer he was more hands on than his predecessor, but he had a big office and occasionally he'd sneak a nap instead of lunch.

It was summer and his sleep schedule was off. He slept when he got home in the afternoon rather than at night. His wife did her thing with the two kids and no one was in the house until nine p.m. That afforded Tom the quietness he needed to get solid sleep.

His hair had turned a lot greyer since taking the new job five months earlier. And at times he felt he was close to retirement. But the truth was he was still a ways off.

He was about to bark out orders again when his phone rang. "That was fast," he said aloud and answered the call. "What's up?"

"Couldn't get the passenger's name," the reporter said. "But check this out. Stewardess is dead and the passenger who did it ... six years old."

Tom spun and moved farther from everyone's earshot. "Are you serious? Is this confirmed?"

"The stewardess portion, yes. Not the kid part. He's a minor. Tom ..." the reporter paused. "The plane was heading to New York."

"Then good thing it's heading back to London."

"No, listen, this is important, I drove Byron's wife and son to the airport this morning. They're on that plane. Tom, Byron's kid is six."

"Jesus," Tom gasped out. "You don't think ..."

"I don't know."

"Keep on it. Do you know if Byron was made aware?"

"None of the families are told yet."

Tom nodded and looked around the room. "Okay, I'll call him before this breaks. Thank you." He slid the phone from his ear and watched the screen as it indicated the call had ended. He hesitated. What would he tell Byron? What could he tell him?

He opted for a filtered truth. Tom would let Byron know the plane was heading back to London and that the stewardess was injured. Because really, that was the only confirmation he had.

Chapter Three

Alexandria, VA

Had Byron not fallen asleep on the couch he wouldn't have heard the phone ring. He put it on the charger in the kitchen and sat on the sofa to watch television. He was out like a light.

Byron never even saw his latest news segment.

When did he start feeling so old? Not that he was, not at all, but he felt it. Jet lag, combined with dealing with his two daughters alone while his wife was still in London. They were feeling better the day before. The girls had caught that same one-day virus as Ren; they fell ill as soon as they arrived home. But when they started to run about, Byron, not feeling like shopping or cooking, took them to the Pizza Haven. Videos games, pizza, a hot spot for energetic kids, and it wiped him out.

The last straw.

Though Alyssa, at nine years old, was old enough to run amuck at the Haven, Byron still chased her. It was packed with kids.

Jade, their oldest, had more fun than any of them and she was thirteen.

But all three of them were exhausted.

How long had the phone rang? How many times.

Seeing the early hour, Byron figured it was his wife saying her flight was delayed. He was just about in the kitchen, just about to answer when he heard a thump above his head.

It was Alyssa's room, and concerned she fell out of bed, Byron went upstairs and would call back the person after he checked on his daughter.

He walked upstairs. As he passed Jade's room, he saw Alyssa at the end of the hall. She just stood there, staring, arms at her side.

"Alyssa, honey, you all right?"

19

Alyssa tilted her head.

He figured she was sleepwalking and he smiled. "Honey, let's go back to bed." He extended his hand to her as he moved her way.

Just as he reached her, he heard the creak of Jade's door. He looked over his shoulder. Jade emerged slowly from her room. "Jade, it's okay, go back to bed, Alyssa is sleepwalking."

A pause. A brief pause and then without warning, Jade sped to her father and jumped for him, sailing her body like a wrestler going off the top rope.

He shrieked in surprise and fell to the floor.

Byron's back slammed hard but he never felt the pain of that fall. Jade's fingers dug into the flesh of his chest, clawing and clawing, rapidly and mad. Digging for a buried treasure of some sort.

He cried out, trying to get up, but Jade's knee pinned against his thigh.

"Alyssa!" he screamed, and tilted his head. From his view on the floor, he saw Alyssa just standing there. "Get help!"

Jade kept clawing. Then, with a hard swing and swoop down, her fingernails ripped across his throat.

Byron knew that was the final blow. He felt the abundance of warm blood flow out. His heart beat rapidly. He could still feel every tear of his skin.

Weakly, with Alyssa in his scope of vision, he called out, "Help."

Alyssa took only a single step forward before she ran down the hall and joined her sister in the brutal attack of their father.

Chapter Four

New York City, NY

Seventeen times, Tom made the attempt to get a hold of Byron, but his phone just rang. He even tried Shelly, but her phone didn't ring. It went directly to voice mail.

He left messages.

"This is Tom. Give me a call. Just checking on you."

Typically he wouldn't be so valiant about calling, but he just had a bad feeling.

"Anything?" he asked his tech. "CDC … Ministry of Health?"

The tech shook his head. "Nothing new. You think …" the tech shook his head again.

"What?" Tom asked.

"Byron or his wife didn't do drugs?"

"Not that I know of, why?"

"Well." The tech shrugged. "Just the kid attacked the stewardess. Last report, it took five people to detain him. Sounds like LSD to me."

"You think the kid accidently dropped acid?"

"Remember those little stamps a while back that looked like kid tattoos?" the tech said. "Big thing with them. Could be the same. In fact, he could have found it in the airport."

With folded arms, Tom nodded. "Could be. Sounds like it."

The assistant producer called out, "Forty seconds. Do I run that segment or pull up the hero dog story?"

Tom thought for a second, but only a second. He nodded as he peered at the monitors. "Run it."

Alexandria, VA

Her flight attendant uniform was crisp and fresh and the wheels of her suitcase clicked against the concrete of her driveway as she walked to the back of her car.

Corrine was on time, in fact early for her day of flying. She had plans to stop for breakfast then get a latte before heading to the airport. All in hopes of cutting out rush hour traffic.

She loaded the small suitcase in the trunk of her car then pulled out her phone. She figured she'd call Marie, who was on the flight with her, and see if she wanted to meet up.

Eyes focused on the phone, Corrine closed the trunk and was just about to press 'send', when she saw the girls through the corner of her eye.

Jade and Alyssa, the girls who lived next door, wandered in their front yard. They weren't playing, walking or running, they seemed to wander aimlessly.

Corrine halted her call. It wasn't the wandering that sent warning flags to her, it was the fact that they were in their nightclothes.

"Jade?" Corrine called out.

Jade didn't answer; she only walked in wide circles.

Aiming her voice to her own home, Corrine called out to her husband Ray. She knew he was on the back patio having coffee. "Ray, come out front."

"Be right there," he replied.

The girls still didn't respond or acknowledge, so Corrine walked to their yard.

Alyssa had her back to Corrine. "Alyssa, honey? You okay?"

The child didn't move, and Corrine crouched down and turned her around, losing all of her breath when she saw the child covered in dried blood from head to toe. "Oh my God, are you okay?" She visually checked her for injuries.

Alyssa stared out blankly as if through Corrine.

Corrine stood and moved to Jade. She didn't need to step far; she could see Jade was covered in blood as well.

"Cor," Ray called out. "What's going …" he stopped. "Oh my God, what the hell? Are they hurt?"

"No." Corrine dialed the phone. "I'm calling the police. They're in shock. Something …" Corrine nodded at the open front door. "Something must have happened."

"I'll go check." Ray walked to the house.

"Be careful," Corrine instructed, then drew her attention to the 911 dispatcher all while keeping her eyes on the girls who had stopped moving and stood perfectly still.

Ray didn't make it too far into the house. A sour smell hit him and five steps up the staircase he saw blood smeared on the wall.

That was enough.

He called out Byron's name several times, when he received no reply, he made his own deductions about what happened.

The blood, the silence, the smell. Something brutal had happened to Byron and the girls had witnessed it and that was why they were in a state of shock.

With all the blood, Ray didn't need to see Byron, he left the house to stay with his wife.

London, England

Eight hours.

Shelly wasn't even in labor that long with Ren. He was an easy baby and even easier toddler. She closed her eyes only dozing off a little. What had happened? The sweet yet hyper child turned into a monster in a matter of seconds.

She and Ren were in a quarantine room at the hospital, she couldn't speak to anyone nor use the phone. They did inform her once they didn't see a virus in Ren's bloodstream they cleared the plane and it was on its way back to the States.

She hoped they had told her husband at least.

No one knew what caused Ren's outburst.

No virus. At first they thought it was a reaction to the cold medicine, but it wasn't. Nor was it an accidental ingestion of drugs.

They were now sticking to the diagnosis of a seizure. Something had caused damage to the brain because the scan was showing similarities to a stroke.

Ren lay in the bed, at first he was sedated then he woke, but he awoke calm and in some sort of 'zoned' state.

He stared outward, barely blinking and not moving.

They kept his arms and legs restrained. Shelly tried to talk to him but didn't receive a response.

Would he be the same? Would he ever again be that child that everyone loved to be around?

Life would never be the same for him, for any of them. Not after what happened.

She stood and stretched her arms and legs, walking to the small window to stare out.

Shelly thought of the stewardess. She wondered if she had family, children. Her heart broke for the tragedy that she somehow felt a responsibility for.

After all, Ren was her son.

"Mommy?"

The soft, scared call of her name caused her to spin from the window and look to the bed.

"Ren." She rushed to the bed. "Baby? Baby, are you okay?"

"Mommy," his voice quivered as he tried to lift his arm. "What did I do? Mommy? Why am I tied?"

"Ren, you're sick."

He shook his head. "No, I'm fine. I want to go home. Why aren't we home?"

Shelly moistened her lips and brought them to her sons head, kissing him. "It'll be okay. I promise." She reached for the call button, summoning the nurse. After the single buzz, she stroked Ren's hair. "It'll be all right."

Ren nodded with a shiver, and then the scared child nodded once more, lowered his head and closed his eyes.

"Ren?" Shelly called his name.

Frightening her, his eyes popped open and immediately he began to angrily thrash in the bed, trying to break free of the restraints, flinging his body in a fight against the straps that bound him.

"Somebody!" Shelly cried out.

Two nurses and a doctor flew into the room. The doctor ordered out to 'sedate him' then turned to Shelly. "What happened?"

Shelly backed up. "He was fine. He was fine for a second. He was fine."

Ren continued to thrash. The intravenous tubing ripped from his arm, and the nurse struggled to get a hold on him.

Finally she succeeded in injecting him.

She backed up a few steps and Ren continued to fight. His groaned out an angry fighting-style growl with each thrash he made.

"It's not working," the nurse said.

The doctor looked to the clock on the wall. "Another minute."

Shelly watched. The medication didn't work like the last time. Ren appeared in pain, crying out as if fighting something inside of him. "Help him," Shelly begged.

"Hit him again," the doctor ordered.

"But, Doctor," the nurse argued. "any more can ..."

"Do it."

The nurse looked to the other and together, both nurses after a battle, managed to inject Ren, again, with sedation.

This time it worked.

The boy stopped moving and quieted down.

Talk commenced in the room between the doctor and Shelly about performing more tests, trying to determine what had caused the seizure.

But the notion of tests would be in vain.

The amount of sedation calmed Ren, but it was too much for his small body.

Within the hour, the six-year-old boy passed away in his sedative induced sleep.

New York City, NY

It felt like the longest day of Tom's life and it was far from over. He wanted to go home, see his wife and rest up before heading back in to work.

And it wasn't just work he had to do.

His eight-year-old daughter was on the sofa watching television and Jill, his wife, was in the kitchen unpacking groceries. She was still in 'work' clothes, a teacher who was getting ready for the start of the new school year.

Jill gave him a surprised look when he walked in the kitchen. She was a slender woman, slightly taller than Tom, and was ageless, he envied that. How she dealt with him all those years, he never knew.

She called him when she saw the broadcast about the incident on the London plane, especially when the news confirmed it was a child who had done the attacking.

It took a while, but Tom was able to confirm it was indeed Byron's son who had caused the incident.

Tom's news agency was the only one with that information, and Tom didn't let it get out. But that wasn't the worst, no sooner did he receive the confirmation, he got a call from the Alexandria police telling him Byron had been brutally murdered in front of the girls.

Shortly after that, his correspondent relayed that Ren had died.

Tom spent his entire afternoon talking to Byron's family, trying to piece things together where authorities were not.

Jill welcomed him home with compassionate and embracing arms. "I'm sorry."

She had known Byron and his family as long as Tom.

Tom nodded. "It's crazy, Jill, totally crazy."

"What did Jeff say? Has he spoken to Shelly?"

"He just picked her up at the hospital. I got all the info. She is a mess." Tom shook his head. "Her son has died, her husband killed … her daughters in some weird state of shock."

"I would think so, after seeing their dad killed."

"No. Jill, I spoke to Byron's mother. The girls are in and out of this shock and when they aren't they exhibit erratic outbursts. Jade attacked a nurse in one of these fits."

Jill tilted her head with a lack of understanding.

Tom held up his hand. "Shelly told Jeff, that was how Ren was. And Byron wasn't killed with a weapon, he was killed by some sort of attack."

Jill stepped back. "Like the stewardess."

"Exactly."

"Tom? You don't think the girls did it, do you?"

"Oh, yeah." Tom nodded, walked across the kitchen and pulled a bottle of bourbon from the cabinet. "Too much of a coincidence. Ren, the girls ... they have this shock behavior and violent outbursts. Something is up. I called the Ministry of Health, the CDC, WHO."

"And?"

"And after call transfer to call transfer, I spoke to someone who took the info."

"What do you think it is?" Jill asked.

"I think the kids caught something, some bacteria that infected the brain. Who knows? I'm not a doctor." He downed his drink. "But there's a link, and I did my part to point it out."

Jill exhaled loudly. "You don't think something odd is happening do you?"

"Like an outbreak?" Tom questioned. "No." He shook his head and poured another drink. "I think this is an isolated, freak occurrence." He took a healthy swig and set down the glass. "Let's hope."

District 3

June 15 – Year 5 P.D.

The voices.

They carried but only in the dead of night. In the wee hours when electric shut down, the hum was gone, that was when they could be heard.

The man believed those on the other side, outside the wall, had no clue that those inside were blocks away.

They were diligent and he knew because when he could, he'd walk those blocks and listen.

Bailey! We love you!

Kristen, we're here!

Be strong!

We are waiting!

So many voices, taking turns to call out. But he didn't reply. He'd walk to the wall, sit down, close his eyes and listen.

His heart broke with each call of a name or holler of love.

At first the area around the wall was nothing but debris but as the years rolled on, the foliage grew. He had tried so many times to figure a way out, but he knew until the electric charges were finished and down, he and the others were stuck behind that wall.

Unlike the others, it was the man's choice to go into District 3.

But it really wasn't a choice—it was something he felt strongly that he had to do. Even though it meant giving up everything in life and the person he loved most.

She was there, he knew it and felt it, she was on the other side of the wall.

He never heard her, but he felt her.

29

How could he not? He had known her forever and loved her that long.

The man sensed her.

Early on, he was uncertain how long she'd stay, because right after the clad iron wall closed, so many people had moved to the other side of the wall.

He found his way to the tallest building in the city, and to the top, he looked, so many stared out the window watching those who waited outside the wall.

He couldn't see her or make out any faces, but he saw the thousands of people. Mere specks and dots.

The man wondered if they ever looked to the windows in the tall buildings. If they did, could they see those who watched the *waiters* every day.

He was one of them.

But going to the wall made him feel closer.

The man had watched as the *waiters* drifted away down to a few. Now, five years post the Divide, there were only a handful. The dutiful.

Again, he knew she was one of them.

Each time he made it to the wall, he was saddened. Filled with a missing and emptiness in his chest. He'd imagine her out there, watching the wall, calling out.

As he did, every time he went to the wall, he placed down a wild flower, and before he went back to his place, he laid his hand flush to the wall, placed his forehead to the concrete and stayed that way for a moment. His eyes closed, lips parted to release a heavy breath, then he whispered, "I love you," before he turned and walked away.

PART TWO: TAG, YOU'RE IT

Chapter Five

August 29

Alexandria, VA

"This is Cyrus Donner of the Centers for Disease Control and Prevention; we're trying to reach Thomas Gibson. Could you please return our call, it's of an urgent matter. At ..."

Tom set down the phone. It wasn't the time to call them back, urgent or not. He had just left the funeral home for the final viewing of Byron and Ren. He had watched the pallbearers escort the adult casket and child casket while an August rain beat down.

No words. Simply no words. Shelly was barely able to stand, her own daughters still in the hospital. No one could speak to her, she made no sense at all, her emotions controlling her to the point she was disoriented.

The little 'funeral flag' was on his car when Tom slid in and took a moment. He had driven from New York the night before, but couldn't sleep. Waiting for everyone to pull out into the procession, he checked his phone. One missed call, the CDC.

After starting his car, turning on his flashers, he placed on the radio, hoping maybe some music would help. It didn't.

The very first thing he heard was a news report regarding a child in Washington, DC, having a violent episode.

Typically, Tom wouldn't think too much of it, but after what Ren had done and then the girls being hospitalized for post-traumatic stress disorder, Tom wondered. Combined with the fact that he missed a call from the CDC, Tom worried. He knew, a part of him just knew, that it wasn't just his area, it wasn't just Ren. Somehow he'd be hearing more news of violent outbursts.

How and why he thought this, he didn't know.

He listened to the message from Cyrus, a name he didn't recognize, and opted for a later call back. In fact, Tom thought about not calling back at all.

A newsman that sought facts, Tom had an inner fear of the situation. Even his wife thought he was overboard.

Gut instinct? Maybe.

But holding on to the 'no news is good news' theory, Tom created his own 'good news' world—by holding off on that call to the CDC.

Chapter Six

August 29

Ripley, WV

Brady Lynn Donner was named after her father who tragically died three hours before she was born. A car accident on the way to the hospital. Of course, 'Donner' wasn't her last name, it was her married name and one she had longer than the maiden.

Who was Brady Donner? She would tell you that she knew exactly who she was. Average looks, height and weight, unless she 'dolled' herself. Something she liked to do and did so often, mostly for weekly date night with her husband.

Ripley, West Virginia, was a small square town. Picture perfect with a hint of modern added to it, some fast-food restaurants and chain-named stores. She didn't hail from Ripley, she didn't even hail from West Virginia. She had moved there less than a month before and still hadn't adjusted.

Brady would tell anyone she had a blessed life. Her mother remarried when she was young. A down-to-earth man of money and means. Ralph was a good guy. Still around, still always there for Brady. Even though her mother had passed when she was a teen, Ralph was still in the picture. He made his money from processed canned meat.

Money that provided Brady a good life. Never a rich brat, but never one who wanted. She often guessed her mother married Ralph for the money and wasn't sure if her mother loved him. But Brady did.

A blessed life.

A good mom, great father figure, and brains. Brady was a computer whiz and started making money at that until, of course, everyone turned into a computer whiz.

She wasn't conventional. She didn't like the having to lead her life by the clock, so anything that helped her work on the go or from home was preferable.

Again, she had the advantage to change careers and not worry about the money. Ralph paid her for inspecting labels or something in his canned meat factory any time she was in between jobs.

When she married Bobby, she was working a few hours a day. Her positioned was replaced by a computer program monitored by a barely-above-minimum-wage guy. She moved to mobile phones and conquered them. Then like computers, so did everyone else.

Ralph told her to think ahead. Think way out of the box. She presented her idea about making really ingenious computer games and programs people can download and play. Ralph told her, people were already doing it, go beyond. What was the next step?

So Brady minimized her programs and was one of the first designers of a phone app.

People thought she was crazy. Who the heck was going to play games on a phone? Phones weren't even built for them.

Then they were.

It wasn't a wide-open field.

She made a lot of money at first, apps sold for a quite a bit, then the freebies came along and she had to lower her prices.

That was how she made her living.

Blessed life.

Her husband was the greatest. She loved him more than the day she met him at Ralph's canned meat factory. That was the summer after high school, when Ralph was trying to find something for Brady to do and he put her in charge of tours.

Tours? At first she thought, who the heck would want to take a tour of a canned meat factory. It wasn't even the big-named canned meat like Spam. It was the underdog. But apparently, Bobby did. He was obsessed with it.

They clicked, they dated, they married. Very few problems, lots of bickering, but otherwise a great marriage. One thing was missing. A child.

Since Brady was able to work a lot from home, they tried. They tried for nearly twenty years. They tried everything, fertility treatments, test after test. Nothing indicated why they couldn't have a child. They were discouraged, especially when Bobby's mom, had that late life, 'whoops, I thought I was in menopause' baby.

Ralph gave them money for in vitro, it took, Brady was carrying triplets. Unfortunately she lost them at 20 weeks and with that, her hope.

She resolved herself to the fact that her blessed life would not be blessed with children.

Then just after their eighteenth anniversary, the one where they didn't even fool around. Eighteen years of marriage, routine lovemaking that cut down to maybe once a week, ended up producing Samantha. They were beyond elated, and Brady's world became Samantha.

So it didn't matter where she lived, as long as she was with her three-year-old daughter and Bobby. That's what she thought, until they moved to Ripley, West Virginia.

There was nothing to do in Ripley. She could go to the diner, but as soon as she walked in, everyone stared at her. Bobby's shop was a block down the road from the diner and municipal building. He got the contract to repair the county vehicles; and that was the reason for moving there, going from a mechanic at a local chain car shop to having his own business.

There was one positive thing about living in Ripley, Brady could walk everywhere. When Bobby didn't answer his phone, she walked to his shop.

Bobby's youngest brother, the menopause baby, now eighteen, had moved with them as well. Why he would do that, Brady didn't know. Bobby's other two brothers were well off.

Then again, Bobby was the oldest and he was a father figure to Perseus.

While Perseus wasn't the most normal of names, he himself was a normal kid. And a great babysitter. In fact all of Bobby's brothers had odd names. Apparently, Bobby's mother became infatuated with Greek tragedies and history after Bobby was born.

She recalled when Ralph heard the name choice for the menopause baby.

"Let me get this straight," Ralph said. "Perseus."

"Yes."

"Perseus, Cyrus, Opus and ... Bob." Ralph whistled. "Well, I can tell which one Carol didn't think was destined for greatness."

Ralph always made Brady giggle. She inherited his sense of humor, or as Bobby called it a 'challenged' sense of humor; she laughed heartedly at knock-knock jokes.

One brother babysitting, one being the reason for the visit, Brady sought out Bobby.

It wasn't too hard. He purchased the full-stocked auto shop and named it *Bob's*.

Not too original, then again, they were in Ripley.

The bay door was open and she spotted Bobby right away, well, his rear. She could tell that rear from anywhere as he bent under that hood. She also spotted that skinny kid that he hired. He wasn't real bright. He also wasn't really a kid either, more like thirty, and for some reason he rubbed Brady the wrong way. What was his name? What was his name?

Tad. That was it.

"Morning, Mrs. Brady," Tad said.

"Really?" She crossed her arms. "Really? Mrs. Brady?"

"That's your name, I'm trying to be respectful."

"My first name is Brady. I have told you this."

"That's weird," he said.

"So is Tad."

"No, it's not."

"Yeah, it is," Brady snapped. "People can make fun of that name. A Tad of this, a tad of that."

"Brady Bunch."

Brady gasped. "You're so rude. Bobby, fire him."

Bobby grumbled and stepped from under the hood. He grabbed a rag from the back of his jeans and wiped his hands. "I'm not firing Tad."

"Then can you give him a *tad* of a hard time."

Bobby forced a smile. He was ruggedly handsome with sprinkles of grey in his dark hair, mainly at the temple and top. Otherwise, like Brady, he was average everything. "What's up? What brings you here?"

"You aren't answering the phone. I thought you were dead."

"No you didn't."

"Okay, I didn't. I think your brother has a thing for me."

"Perseus? That would be weird," Bobby replied.

"Not Perseus. The other one, he keeps calling."

"Which other one?" Bobby asked.

"Cyrus. He called sixteen times. Why in the world is he calling sixteen times?"

"Why don't you answer the phone and find out."

Brady waved out her hand. "I hate talking on the phone."

"Then send him a text."

"I did, and he replied to answer the goddamn phone."

"Then answer it." Bobby sighed out heavily. "I have to get back to this truck. Why don't you walk around town and try to make friends."

Brady laughed, causing a weird noise across her lips as she did. "Friends? You can't make friends in three weeks."

"Yeah, you can. I did."

"That's you."

"Go to the diner, the library, mingle."

"Oh my God. Please."

"Brady, I don't have time."

"You should make time," she said. "You dragged me here. And for the record, you promised me a better life."

"Well, your father is the king of canned meat; I can't get much better than that."

"True." Brady bobbed her head back and forth. "But this is not better."

"I now own my own business. How do you figure?"

"It's West Virginia. We lived in Ohio. I'm pretty sure moving from Ohio to West Virginia is not a step up."

From across the garage, Tad hollered out, "Actually it's southeast."

"Oh." Brady grunted. "Go back under a car or something."

"Brady, go home. Go somewhere. Just go," Bobby instructed.

"What about your brother?"

"He doesn't have a thing for you. Next weekend is Labor Day and my brothers are all coming down."

"No, Ralph is coming that …"

"Then it will be a great weekend." Bobby darted a kiss to her cheek. "Go."

"Fine. Do you want me to bring you lunch?"

Bobby shook his head. "I'll hit the diner."

"Ug, they hate me in there."

"They don't hate you, they just don't know you," Bobby said. "And maybe … don't take this the wrong way. Maybe if you weren't such a snob?" He raised an eyebrow.

Brady gasped. "How am I not supposed to take that the wrong way?"

Bobby shrugged. "I got to work. See ya. And, Brady?"

"Yeah."

"Answer my brother's calls, okay?"

"Fine." Arms still folded, just for the heck of it, Brady gave a glare to Tad and turned. She'd think about answering Cyrus' calls. But she couldn't figure out what would be so important that he had to blow-up her phone. Had she taken a moment to

39

remember where he worked, then perhaps Brady would have thought more of it. But somehow, she never connected Cyrus to the Centers for Disease Control, only to her family.

Curse of the Innocents

Alexandria, VA

Alyssa and Jade had killed their father. Brutally took his life, yet no one came out and said so. There were those who believed they had done the deed. Those who were checking the skin fragments under Jade's nails.

But who wanted to admit the truth. Who would want to believe that two girls would tear apart their father and play with his intestines like a jump rope before snapping into some sort of catatonic and mild state. Unremorseful and unknowledgeable of what they did.

The truth would come out, but not until after another tragedy. They were detained in a children's psychiatric ward for violent outbursts. They had been checked for seizures, viruses, anything that could explain the sudden behavior change.

Nothing.

They were a case study nightmare. There was no evidence to indicate if they were sick prior, the only one who knew was dead.

But the bank knew something. Authorities found a receipt for a children's pizza place, where kids could be kids and get infected by other kids.

The CDC rushed on that. Even though there was no biological proof of infection, they didn't take a chance and started tracking down all those who would have been at the Pizza Haven.

Local police scrambled about the town looking for the person who tore apart Byron. Neighbors locked themselves inside fearful of the madman. When all along, the culprits were secured.

Nurses in the unit complained about them. They made noises and reacted too violently to treat, but when Helen Boyle showed up, they were fine.

She hated leaving her daughter Shelly at the funeral, but Helen couldn't take it anymore. She lost her grandson, her son-in-law and her granddaughters were locked away

It broke her heart, looking through the observation window at her two young granddaughters. A white padded room, both girls wearing only gowns and restrained.

It was for their safety and the safety of the nurses, Helen was told.

But the seventy-year-old woman was tough and insisted on seeing the girls. Talking to them.

Where was the catatonic state? Where were the lost stares? The girls were talking and looked scared. None of what Helen witnessed matched what she was told. These were her flesh and blood, her grandchildren. She had no fear of them.

Finally, after many arguments, they let her in to see the girls and immediately, Alyssa and Jade reached unsuccessfully to their grandmother.

"Babies, oh my babies." Helen reached for them, embracing the girls as best as she could.

"Grammy," Jade wept, "we're scared. I'm scared. Why are we here?"

"Sweetie." Helen laid her hand on Jade's face. "You're not well. You …" Her eyes shifted to the leather restraints on Jade's arm. On the right wrist they were torn and frayed, almost separated. "What is this?" She reached down.

Jade said nothing.

"Honey, your strap." It struck Helen as odd. If they were going to restrain the girls then surely, they would have been restrained with straps that weren't imperfect.

The second her fingers swiped across the damaged restraint, Jade whipped out her hand at full force and snapped free from the restraint. Before Helen could register what was going on,

Jade's hand went instantly to Helen's face. Her fingers seared immediately into Helen's eye sockets, deep and hard.

Helen screamed.

Alyssa screamed too but not for the same reason. She screamed and struggled to get at Helen, as well.

Screams of agony carried in the room, as Jade's fingers clawed mercilessly into Helen's face, tearing at the skin, ripping it from her easily, like peeling an orange.

Helen was not without a fight. She grabbed on to Jade's hand, trying to free herself, but her attempts were in vain. Jade's determination carried more strength than Helen had.

By the time help had entered the room, which wasn't long, Helen was a dangling being, hanging from the fingertips of a maddened young girl.

Chapter Seven

August 29

Alexandria, VA

The funeral procession ran from the last viewing at the funeral home, to the church, then cemetery, then finally the reception or wake.

It was a long procession and an even longer day. Tom had plans to drive back to New York, but was thinking of getting a room.

There was just something about attending the funeral of a child. Ren was not much younger than his daughter and looking at that little white coffin was the hardest thing Tom ever had to do. He watched the video tribute to Byron and Ren as it played to some 'life goes on but I remember you' type of song. Anything and everything to pull at the heartstrings and it did.

The news station took care of the reception so Shelly didn't have to worry. Before going on, Tom called his wife, Jill, just to see how her and the kids were doing.

Tom had spent a good deal of time on the road early in their marriage, but this trip was heart wrenching.

Jill told him that maybe it was best that he didn't make the trip home, and for him to rest. She'd find him a room somewhere. Then before she ended the call, she told him that a man named Cyrus Donner called.

Tom would call him back, but after he checked into the room.

The funeral reception was held a hotel restaurant; it was filled with typical post-funeral chatter.

44

I heard he had seizures.
Those poor girls had to see Byron get killed.
Where are the girls?
I heard they were sick.

Whispers of the events and questions regarding them were plenty during the reception.

Before the meal was served, Tom went to the bar and got a drink. He needed one.

He watched Shelly. Bourbon in hand, straight up, he watched her. Tom admired her strength. Greeting people, trying to smile, but he could see the pain. He wouldn't be able to do it. Not at all. Being at funerals always made him think of how he'd handle death and mortality. And then something happened.

She was handed a phone. Who would call her at the wake of her husband and son? Downing more of his drink, Tom saw her face go from drawn to horrified. She gasped so loud, it was almost a scream, dropped the phone and hand over her mouth, ran out.

Tom wanted to find out what happened, but enough people followed Shelly, calling her name, trying to stop her. Apparently, it was another round of bad news. More than likely it was the girls. As if her life hadn't already taken a horrific and tragic turn, he couldn't see how she could possibly handle any more.

On those thoughts, Tom ordered another drink.

Mon City, Pa

The eviction notice was visible on the front door of her trailer home before Nola Carson even stepped from her car. She expected it to come, nonetheless her heart sunk when she saw it.

45

NODDING – JACQUELINE DRUGA

Ignoring it wouldn't make it go away. She didn't have the option to move, not at all.

She could juggle the water bill, she wouldn't need propane until late fall, rob Peter to pay Paul was an option to delay the eviction; it would take a miracle for Nola to get a step ahead.

Her old beat-up van did that putter and bang just before she shut it off. She said a short prayer that it started in the morning.

She didn't live in the best trailer court, but it was the most affordable, and all her neighbors were nice and helpful.

The trailer was perfect. It was handicap accessible and Nola needed that for her fifteen-year-old son, Eddie.

Life wasn't ever easy for Nola. At one point it was better and then it all went downhill and she had been doing everything she could to stay afloat.

Fate dealt her a raw deal but Nola never looked at it as such. Yes, there were times she just curled up and cried, but she pulled it together, she had to, she had three children who depended on her.

Everything was second to her children. Nola would say she used to be pretty. Time, however, aged her and she looked like a woman in her forties rather than one in her thirties. Her weight wasn't the best; it had been two years since she had a professional haircut. She trimmed her own hair with the ponytail method. And she couldn't recall the last time she got a new pair of jeans from a place other than a thrift store.

None of that mattered to Nola as long as her children had a home and food. That's what was important.

It was never her intention to be a welfare mother or statistic. She got pregnant at seventeen. While she didn't get married, she finished school. Her boyfriend Ed, the baby's father, joined the service and they married right after.

He tried. She tried, they both did. They sacrificed to make ends meet. It was hard on Nola to keep a job because they were always moving or Ed was getting deployed. Then when their son

Eddie was ten, he was hit by a car. Ed was overseas, Nola was pregnant with Carlie and Ben was only two.

She was in Texas the year Eddie was in the hospital. He was never able to walk again or have full use of his left arm. But he was alive, her son was alive and that was all that mattered to Nola.

It was a lot of adjustments in life, but they learned and succeeded.

The medical bills stacked up, not to mention the need for home equipment.

After Ed returned home, he went into recruiting for more stability, and after training, they moved to Pennsylvania. They found a home that was handicap accessible. Everything looked brighter until Ed went out after work for a drink with his coworkers.

All the deployments, tours in war zones, and Ed was shot breaking up a fight.

Shot and killed.

Nola's brother urged her to move in with him and his wife, their house was large enough and they'd make the home repairs for Eddie. Nola refused. She could do it.

But apparently by the eviction notice, she wasn't.

After Ed's death, she was unable to afford the home and she moved into the trailer with the three kids.

She did okay, working at the Laundromat, living off of that and Social Security from Ed. The insurance money went to pay medical bills so collectors would stop harassing her, and she had to buy the van. The car payment on the special van was too much.

There were so many days she just wanted to pack the kids and drive to her brother's house. He wouldn't mind, neither would his wife. But her van wouldn't make it. It barely made it across town some days to take the kids to school or take Eddie to the doctors.

Plus her pride was there. She didn't want anyone to know she was failing.

Before stepping out of the van, she told Ben and Carlie to hold on, and she pulled her checkbook from her purse. She had to pay the caretaker. She wrote out a check. It left her twelve dollars.

Nola groaned and opened her van door. "Let's go."

Ben and Carlie raced around to the house and up the ramp.

"Hey," Ben called out. "There's a letter on the door. Notice of ..."

"I got it. I got it." Nola ripped it down, wishing he didn't know how to read so well for a seven-year-old. "Don't worry about it. Go." She opened the door. Her children were happy and carefree, and that made Nola happy. They darted into the house.

The video game sounds were loud when Nola walked in, and Eddie was positioned in front of the television.

Ben hurriedly dropped his book bag and sat by his brother. "Can I play?"

"Let me finish this," Eddie replied.

Eddie, so bright, handsome, and smart too; he had a good heart and never let his disability get him down. Nola planted a kiss on his head.

"I see you finished your work," she said.

"Yep," Eddie replied, more focused on playing the game.

Nola was tired, really tired, she just wanted to sit down and relax but knew that would be impossible. She laughed when Carlie announced loudly as she ran, that she had to pee.

Then Sharon came from the back hall of the trailer. Sharon was Eddie's caretaker, an older woman, thick around the middle, who lived in the trailer court. She had been a nurse's aide for years with dementia patients, but that wore her down emotionally and physically.

"We had a good day," Sharon announced. "Smell him. I finally convinced him to shower."

Eddie replied to her comments, intermittently while playing. "I ... don't do ... anything. Why do I need ... to shower ever ... day. Darn."

Nola smiled and faced Sharon. "Thank you. One less thing I have to fight with him about." She then handed Sharon the check. "Here you go."

Sharon hesitated. "Hey ... um ... look. I love Eddie. I ... if you wanna hold off ..."

"No, we're good. Take it." Nola extended the check farther.

"It's not important, okay?" Sharon said. "It really isn't."

"You have a family."

"I do." Sharon exhaled. "But ... you have been good to me. Hold on to the check. Please. Sam hit the daily and we got that extra cash this week. Plus, he's been working a lot of overtime."

Nola just stared at Sharon.

"I mean it. I've been there, Nola. We've been there." Sharon ignored the check and walked to the door. "This week's on me." She passed a smile to Nola and walked out.

The second the door closed, Nola felt a thickness hit her throat and her eyes burned as they glossed over. She looked down at the check and her vision blurred as tears welled. Folding the check, she thought of what Sharon just did and Nola's lips puckered.

Don't cry. Don't cry. She told herself.

Then ...

"Sharon's pretty cool," Eddie said. "She gave me her son's old superman tee shirt."

"Yeah," Nola said breathlessly. "Sharon is very cool." She choked on the final word and folded the check at the same time she folded. She squeezed tight to the corners of her eyes as if it would stop the tears. A simple gesture, a sacrifice from Sharon, just overwhelmed her.

"Mommy?" Carlie's tiny voice questioned. "Are you crying? Are you okay?"

"Yeah. Yeah." Nola sniffed and pulled Carlie's tiny frame into her. "Mommy's fine. I'm fine."

Nola *was* fine. She was broke, sore, and tired, but fine. She may not have had it easy, but she had good friends, a roof over her head, food on the table, and more importantly, her children were healthy and happy.

It wasn't a perfect life, but it was better than fine.

Alexandria, VA

Shelly was done … completely done.

She sat at the kitchen counter, laptop before her and penned an e-mail to Tom Gibson. It was long, but she had to get it out and Tom was the best person for the information.

Something was up, something bigger than anyone knew. She was a part of it from the beginning or at least close to the beginning. Watching her sweet and innocent six-year-old son, bare handedly rip apart a flight attendant—crushed her. Then to hear her husband died the same way. Shelly didn't care what the police said. She suspected her daughters.

Suspected that they too had the same seizures as Ren; seizures brought on by some sort of flu. And the girls had the flu. They just recovered and made it home before Ren.

Her suspicions were confirmed when she received the call at the wake. Her mother was in critical condition. The girls, Jade specifically, had attacked her.

Shelly was already an emotional mess torn apart inside from all that happened. They told her how badly her mother was injured. Helen would never be the same. Her face was gone, torn away, eyes gouged out. Not ten minutes at the hospital, not a moment after getting the news that her mother would survive,

50

Helen went into violent seizures. Unlike the children, her body convulsed as some sort of white foamy substance oozed from the bandages, her body flopping up and down, head thrashing, and everything shaking. The staff didn't even have a moment to give her something … Helen died.

That fast.

Maybe thirty seconds from the start of the convulsion.

It was the final straw for Shelly. She was done. She lost her son, her husband, her mother, and in a sense, she lost her daughters. They would never be the same.

All that went into her letter.

She finished the e-mail to Tom with a certain amount of internal peace. Shelly had stopped crying and didn't feel sad any longer, she felt relieved. It would be over soon.

After hitting 'send', Shelly reached to the revolver on the counter, placed it into her mouth and without hesitation, pulled the trigger.

For Shelly it was over.

Chapter Eight

Atlanta, GA

Cyrus Donner was a stoner. For as long as he could remember he smoked weed. He'd steal it from his father knowing full well, his father would never say it was missing. Cyrus also was never blamed for it—his brother Bob was—but not Cyrus. After all, who would suspect the President of the Future Scientists of America to be a pothead?

One time his younger brother Opus even tried to rat him out in defense of Bobby. But his father didn't buy it and both brothers got in trouble for trying to pull a conspiracy against poor Cyrus.

Cyrus wasn't a poor Cyrus. He was brilliant. He was President of the Future Scientists because he knew he was going to be one. He didn't want to be a doctor, but he knew if he wanted to get into medical microbiology, he'd have to. He loved diseases. Obsessed with them.

He trudged through his medical internship at University of Pittsburgh. He thought it was trudging, but the chief of staff called him the Einstein of medicine. Offered him a position, to which, Cyrus said, "nah."

He finished his degree in microbiology and landed a field job with a pharmaceutical company working on new drugs. That was where he wanted to be. Studying the microbes and killing them—or anything else that invaded the body.

For his thesis, he was exceptionally high. He binged smoked when he wrote it, he hated writing papers and he penned what he himself called a 'fiction meets reality piece'.

It was a piece on the potential mutation of the *Onchocerca volvulus* a microscopic nematode carried by the black fly. People weren't aware of how common and problematic the black fly was all over the world. So much so, that agricultural departments tried to curb their population for public safety. He wrote about the possible mutation in the nematode that caused river blindness and other things. He called his thesis *The Invisible Foe that could bring on the Apocalypse in thirty days or less.*

Cyrus really didn't take it seriously. Neither did his professors, barely giving it a C only because Cyrus was too brilliant to fail over a poorly written and outlandish thesis.

He put that thesis out of his mind, moved on to the pharmaceutical dream job. On a whim he applied to the World Health Organization and they rejected him. Several months later he was hired by the CDC, an offer he couldn't resist financially and professionally.

He was going to be hands on with all those level four nematodes.

Sweet. The only problem was he had to dodge those pesky random drug screenings. Actually, it wasn't a problem. He invented something to take.

Living the life.

Then it got weird. Not even a week earlier, the CDC and WHO were getting bombarded with calls from one man. Tom Gibson of WNN. He wasn't just a reporter; he was the head news honcho. Tom called once, then after a few hours, he called over and over again, only stopping after three days.

Cyrus found out about his calls at the same time his thesis came back to haunt him.

"Mr. Gibson from the World News Network was calling insistently," the Director told Cyrus in his office.

Cyrus didn't really understand why he was in the Director's office, he wasn't that big of a deal at the CDC, he was buried in a lab. So why tell him about Tom?

Then the Director continued, "We couldn't figure out why he was calling, because there was nothing on our plate. No indication. By the time he stopped calling, things were happening and rather fast. It was actually a tip he left us that started our discovery."

Thinking, *Okay, what's this have to do with me?* Cyrus just nodded.

Then he got his answer.

"Tom stopped calling. And I discovered this." The Director dropped a printed copy of his thesis to the desk.

"Aw, man," Cyrus whined. "I knew that would come back to haunt me. Listen when I wrote that, I was—"

"Brilliantly insightful," the Director cut him off and finished the sentence.

"What?"

"I believe … we believe … this is happening."

"You're shitting me?" Cyrus grabbed the thesis. "The OV has mutated?"

"A form of it, yeah. We can't be sure, that's where you come in. If it is a mutated OV, that would explain a lot. And it connects a lot of dots."

"I'm lost."

"You won't be." The Director handed him a folder. "Incidents are in there. Specimens are being shipped in. I need you to lead an in-house team on this ASAP. Positively identify it as the source, and come up with every possible theoretic outcome based on science. More importantly, you have to come up with a solution. Because according to your thesis, it can't be beat."

Cyrus chuckled. "Yeah, well, my thesis was a bunch of made-up, over-the-top bull to get it over with."

"Yeah, well, your 'over-the-top' bull thesis is spot on. And if we don't do something about it now, your 'thirty days or less' prediction …" the Director took on a serious tone, "will become a reality."

Alexandria, VA

Under normal circumstances, Tom would be drunk. He had consumed that much alcohol. But his emotional state took control and the alcohol did nothing.

He had a light dinner at the hotel restaurant, and despite the fact that he wasn't feeling like doing much, he still had a news station to run. He powered up his laptop, drew in a connection to the Internet and immediately began downloading his e-mails.

As they loaded, he noticed the news ticker on his desktop. *Accidental consumption of Bath Salts causes violent behavior in DC child.*

They shot him.

Eight years old and they shot the boy because they couldn't calm him down. The officer who pulled the trigger was distraught because he was aiming for an 'injury' shot.

Thinking, *What the fuck?* Tom took another drink. As he set his phone next to his laptop, preparing to check out his e-mails, he thought of the call he missed earlier. Figuring it was late and he'd get a machine, Tom returned the call to the CDC. He didn't feel like talking, but also didn't feel like being the new man who didn't return calls.

He was surprised when after two rings, someone answered.

"This is Cyrus," the male voice said. It was raspy and tired sounding.

Tom stuttered. He didn't expect an answer and especially didn't expect a direct line. "I … um, am returning your call. Tom Gibson."

"Oh yeah, hey, Tom. Thanks."

Silence.

Tom cleared his throat. "Did you call me for a reason?"

55

"Sorry, I was reading something in one of your messages. Yes. You called several days ago, first to see if there were any reports of viruses or bacteria outbreaks causing violent seizures."

"Yes, I did. One of my newsman, his son was the boy on the London flight, that attacked the stewardess."

"The same man whose daughters killed him."

"Um ... I hadn't heard they were the ones. Last I heard the police were—"

"They did it. It isn't public yet, it will be. Anyhow—"

"Dr. Donner, are you always so unaffected?"

"I'm sorry, yes, I am, I'll try to be better. I apologize. I'm calling because your agency sent this man overseas. Can you forward a list of all the locations that he visited?"

"He went to three continents and eight countries. I'll get that information to you as soon as I return to the office."

"I'd appreciate it. I'd also appreciate anything that comes across your desk that is remotely like the Turner incidents. I know health officials don't always get everything if there is another explanation."

"Like the bath-salts boy in DC today?" Tom asked.

"I'm sorry?"

"See, an eight-year-old boy attacked someone, they said he got a hold of bath salts."

"Hence, reiterating what I just said. We don't get it. Thank you for that and anything else you come across. I'll let you go, and I look forward to that information."

"Dr. Donner ..."

"Cyrus please, call me Cyrus."

"Cyrus, if this boy in DC had a virus or something wouldn't the coroner or someone see it immediately in his blood?"

Cyrus laughed.

"That's funny?"

"Yeah, it is, to me. Because what I work with, unless you know what to look for, you wouldn't know it was there."

"What exactly do you look for?"

56

"Pathogenic microbes."

"I have no idea what that is," Tom said.

"Let's say they can be bad."

"I'll look them up. But I appreciate you being free with our responses."

"No problem, I appreciate your help. And why hide anything, it doesn't do any good, right?"

"Right." Tom reached for his drink. "Can I establish a point of contact with you, Cyrus, if this thing needs to get out?"

"For the news?"

"And my family."

"Yes," Cyrus told him.

Tom ended the call, still not knowing how to process the conversation he just had with the doctor. He would look up the 'microbe' thing and more into the child from DC. As he turned back to his computer, he saw the e-mail from Shelly.

At first glance he expected it to be a thank-you for all the station had done, but no sooner did he open it and read the first two lines he knew exactly what it was, and by far it wasn't what he expected.

Tom didn't take the time to read the 'why', he would have plenty of time for that, at that moment he was concerned with Shelly and he immediately called her in case he was mistaken.

It went straight to voice mail.

Sick to his stomach and feeling the bourbon creep back up his esophagus, Tom exercised is only option and called 911.

Curse of the Innocents

September 4

Alexandria, VA

Sergeant Andrews immediately cringed when the domestic disturbance call came in from Mountain Drive. His first thought was *What is up with this street?* In the previous two weeks he had been to the street three times. Of course, all three of those calls were for the Turner family.

This call only indentified a disturbance on the street. Andrews picked up the pace, but didn't put on his lights. That was, until he was a block away.

Was he imagining things? He swore he heard screams and glass breaking. It was the middle of the afternoon. What was happening on the sleepy suburban street?

Mayhem.

He flicked on his lights and sirens the second he turned the bend. People ran in the street and he didn't know where to start. Was there a fire? What the hell was happening? He slowed down and glanced left to a man in his front yard, his face buried in his hands. The man looked distraught.

Andrews hit the brakes and just as he did—

Slam!

"Help me!" A woman stood before the squad car, her hands on the hood. The woman's face was bloody and her shirt saturated with blood as well. "Help me please."

No sooner did Andrews reach for the door, something shot past the right of his peripheral vision, sailing into the woman and sending her from his view. Whatever it was, was small.

With urgency he flung open his door and saw the woman on the ground. She cried out, loud and shrill. On top of her was a child no older than six. The little girl's hands moved fast and

58

furiously in a doggie-paddle motion, ripping into the woman's chest with every stroke. As if scratching away her skin.

Andrews pulled his gun.

He called for the child to stop. Quit. He reached for the child but could not pull the girl from the woman. The child would not cease. Andrews didn't want to shoot the child, he really didn't. The woman had gone motionless and her head tilted right, eyes wide open.

He gagged and coughed into the back of his hand as he aimed. Even though the woman was dead, the child was relentless and continued as if her torso contained a prize in the bottom of a cereal box.

Andrews tried to shoot, but he couldn't. He just couldn't shoot the small child. He had a daughter the same age.

Opting for backup, Andrews inched to his squad car. Just as he slid inside, he felt the searing pain to his left bicep. He looked. Another child had locked his jaws on Andrews' arm.

Instinctively he fought, coldcocking the child in the head. The boy fell immediately to the ground and Andrews, bleeding heavily, got in the car. Blood poured from his wound as he shut and locked the door.

What he witnessed was unbelievable and he didn't have a clue on how to call it in.

It wasn't just the one child that killed the woman, or the boy who bit him. There were several children running amuck madly on the streets. They attacked people, one stood on a car hood swinging his fist down on to the car, one strike after another.

Andrews radioed for backup, for help, for something. The dispatcher had a tone of disbelief when he said what was going on. But the frantic tone of Andrews' voice broke through.

He backed up and withdrew from the street until more officers arrived; he needed to tend to his wound.

It was deep and an entire chunk was missing from his arm.

How the ordeal played out, Andrews would never know. Not fifteen minutes later, he convulsed violently and died in his patrol car.

Chapter Nine

September 4

New York City, NY

Jill Gibson had just finished prepping student folders for the first day of school after Labor Day weekend. Her classroom was just about ready when the text from her husband came.

'Turn on the news.'

It was odd and Tom never sent a text unless something serious was going on. She figured it was his news station he wanted to her watch. The second she turned to WNN, she saw the 'breaking news'. An aerial view showed a suburban street that looked like a war zone. The ticker tape told how six people were dead and several children were being hospitalized.

Jill turned up the volume.

In the fifth such attack in as many days, authorities are now calling it the largest domestic terror strike in history. Believing that newest candy sensation, Razzle Rocks, have been tainted and are causing these episodes that are nothing short of a nightmare for parents.

"Jesus," Jill whispered, and then in a panic, immediately dialed Tom.

"Jill," Tom answered the phone. "You're watching the news, I take it."

"Oh my God, Tom."

"I know. It's crazy. The kids are just nuts. They're calm now, just kind of meandering."

"Well, they came down from that drug. Thank God it didn't kill them. Thank God I refused to let our kids eat that crap."

"No, Jill," Tom said. "Do you know where that shot is from?"

"I'm going to assume, DC, wasn't that the last episode?"

"No, that street is Byron and Shelly's street."

Jill nearly dropped the phone. "The girls. Ren. They probably had that candy."

"It's not the candy."

"But the news said …"

"The news is wrong."

"Tom." Jill chuckled nervously. "You are the news."

"And that is all I can deliver to the public because that's all I have proof of. Authorities say it's the candy. I just am waiting."

"For?"

"Facts and answers."

Jill reached for a chair and slowly sat. "What are you talking about, Tom?"

"Ren and the girls had whatever these kids have. More will have it. I'm waiting for deliverable facts and answers. I can't give the American public any facts, unless I can follow up with answers on what they can do."

"Tom, you're scaring me."

"Good because I am getting scared. Until then, the kids do not leave the house; they don't go to school, play with their friends. Nothing. Understand."

Jill wished Tom could see her face because she just shook her head. "This is ridiculous. It's in Virginia. It's not here. Not in New York."

"You're right. It's not in New York … yet. But it will be." Tom paused. "God help us when it arrives."

Mon City, PA

It would get better. That was what Nola told the landlord when she gave him one hundred and seventy-five dollars. It would get better. He nodded, a good man who completely understood. She told him school would be starting the next week and she wouldn't have to pay for a caretaker for Eddie.

He expressed to her, evicting her wasn't what he wanted to do, but he only owned the trailer, the lot was where the eviction came from.

It barreled over Nola when he said to give it to the trailer court, he could wait. Nola felt she didn't deserve the kindness of others, and it all overwhelmed her.

Her brother called, but she didn't answer. He always sensed when something was up and Nola did not want to be in the position to lie to him or tell him the truth. If she told him the truth, he'd help out and that wasn't what she wanted.

She was done with her work at the Laundromat, picked up the Carlie and Ben from Miss Betty's house, the woman from church who watched them, and was home well ahead of schedule.

It was going to be a good day. After shopping, gas and putting aside what little she needed until next pay, she had forty-two dollars left out of her check and was going to visit the Wal-Mart that night and hoped to get all the kids at least one new shirt for school and some new socks.

Bottom Dollar Grocer, along with their really cool coupons, provided her with a weekend of meals for ten dollars. In fact, with all the sales, the ten dollar and fifty-six cent total tab was going to be like a feast at Nola's house.

Ben and Eddie were in their typical mid-day video game frenzy. Nola tried to talk Ben into going out and playing. Fall was approaching, who knew how many nice days were left.

Carlie was just outside playing with the neighbor Gio. They always played together. On this day, they were in the patch of

NODDING – JACQUELINE DRUGA

grass in clear view of the kitchen window as Nola prepared a meal. She kept peeking out, checking on them. They were building something, running around, playing, yelling.

Washing potatoes, Nola peeked out to see Carlie staring at Gio. Gio was his knees, head down, looking as if he stared at something.

He didn't move.

Thinking nothing much of it, Nola grabbed and rinsed another potato and peeked out.

Still the same.

Third potato, she heard Carlie calling Gio's name.

Fourth potato, it began.

Little girls, without a doubt, scream. They scream when they are happy, scared, angry, for attention, they scream. Loud, long, shrill, top of their lungs, but a mother always can tell when the scream signifies something is wrong.

Carlie made such a scream.

For certain Nola thought she was hurt, looked out the window to see Gio dragging Carlie by the hair. He moved in mad circles and dragged.

"Oh my God." Not even shutting off the sink, Nola flew outside.

Somewhere in her fast escape to go to her daughter's rescue, Eddie asked if Carlie was all right, but Nola just flew outside.

"Gio! Stop!" Nola screamed.

Gio did.

He immediately froze, his hand released Carlie and the little girl seized her opportunity and scurried from the ground. Crying, holding her hair, she raced to the house.

"Run, Mommy, run."

Nola looked over her shoulder with a 'huh?', and fully planned to scold Gio once more, then take him right over to his trailer. By the time she turned her head back to Gio, the six-year-old, had spun her way. He stared with a maddened look.

Nola watched the news. She heard about the tainted candy and that was the first thing that raced into her mind. Gio had eaten that candy. The authorities urged anyone experiencing a Tantrum child, to stay clear and with everything she had, she ran back to her trailer.

She made it to the ramp before Gio leapt at her, landing on his stomach and grabbing her ankle.

She shook her leg and tried to free the boy from her. She wasn't having any luck. His hand had her ankle, fingers gripping into her socks. Any harder, she swore he'd draw blood.

Nola screamed and wouldn't have gotten free had Ben not raced out and with all his might, kicked Gio in the arm.

Gio's grip loosened, and Nola, feeling the freedom, raced into her home, as did Ben.

Gio didn't stay down long. The second the door closed, Nola watched through the window as the tiny boy headed to the door. He didn't stop. SLAM ... Gio bodily hit against it. He rushed the door, banging into it, in a repeated manner. He was determined and diligent. Smashing into the metal door as if his body could break through.

It didn't faze him that he wasn't making progress or that he was bleeding, he just kept coming.

Carlie was crying.

Eddie commented about the candy.

And Nola, after thanking her son, grabbed hold of Carlie and did the only thing she could think of. She called the police.

Atlanta, GA

A text that read 'Possible Case in PA' prompted Cyrus Donner to call Tom, moments before his plane was called to board.

He had called Tom quite a bit.

Typically, Cyrus would have found out about an incident after a medical professional called it in. That was after the police arrived, after transport, but because of Tom, Cyrus was finding out about it before the child was even examined at the hospital. This enabled him to call ahead, make arrangements and set things in motion.

Tom's network of people that monitored police scanners, paid off.

The quaint street in Alexandria was still under child siege when Donner had a team en route. Had Tom not called him, he wouldn't have been so on the ball.

Because of that, Cyrus vowed Tom would be the first to know.

"The kid …" Tom coughed and choked on his words. "He hit against the door of a trailer until he killed himself. They're still on scene. Got this from a Pittsburgh affiliate."

Cyrus exhaled. "Any idea where they are taking him?"

"Probably Mon Valley Hospital."

It wasn't a name Cyrus recognized, neither was the town for that matter and he could only figure the small-town hospital didn't have the resources to deal with things. "I have a team in Pittsburgh," Cyrus said. "I'll get them there. Thank you."

"Seems to be one every day."

"Yeah, well, lucky for us we aren't in Canada."

"I haven't heard anything."

"It's bad there. Did you tell your wife about being cautious?"

"In so many words."

"Good. Good. I haven't a clue what all is going to happen. I have a meeting with the federal government Tuesday; I'll let you know what they have planned. Right now, they are boarding my plane. I'll check my phone as soon as I land."

"Trotting off to follow the illness?" Tom asked.

"No, to see my family. I need to see them, even for a day. I need to. I have a niece."

Tom's exhale carried over the line. "See them before it gets ahead of us?"

"My dear new friend, I believe it already is ahead of us. We just don't know the extent." Cyrus ended the call, put his phone on 'airplane mode' and boarded the plane. He wanted to keep the events out of his mind when he visited his family, but how could he? They would affect his family and the tragic events that cascaded out of control daily were all he could think about.

Charleston, WV

There wasn't much in Ripley to choose from as far as fine eatery went. They had the diner, but Brady knew that Ralph would only settle for them for breakfast and possibly lunch. She had to go on the Internet to find a steakhouse.

Ralph liked his steaks.

She wasn't getting answers from anyone in Ripley. Bobby asked around. Questioning his newfound Ripley friends on where he could get a great steak. Their responses were Outback, Long Horn, and Applebee's.

Really? Was Brady's reaction. You cannot have the King of Canned Ham meat product eat at Applebee's.

So she found a quaint place, great reviews, higher-end prices and a nice menu. The pictures on the net looked good and the restaurant was in a historical location. An old railroad station.

She had her fingers crossed.

Since Cyrus was flying into Charleston—Ripley didn't have an airport—what better place to meet.

Ralph looked like a Texan; in fact he was originally from Texas. Big and thick, wide chest and a gut that was hard as a rock and hung over his too-tight belt. His nose was always red and Ralph always laughed and smiled.

He drove from Ohio, not a far drive at all. He, Opus, and Cyrus would stay with Brady and Bobby in their four bedroom, simple frame home. No hotels needed, it was a family weekend.

Ralph met them at restaurant and greeted them with a hearty hello and embrace. Even Bobby, Opus, and Perseus, they were his family. Brady, even at her average size, was buried in his broad hold.

She adored Ralph.

"Pappy?" Samantha was so excited to see him. "You bring me a surprise?"

"Absolutely, darling." Ralph swept up the little one in his arms. Her long dark hair trailed over his forearm, and he peered at her as if she were the most precious commodity. "I brought everyone a surprise. Where is Cyrus?"

"Uncle Cyrus late."

"Everything all right?" Ralph questioned, balancing Samantha on his hip. "Cyrus is never late."

"Work," Brady answered.

Bobby glanced at his watch. "Let's go sit, get some drinks and wait. His flight landed already so he should be here soon."

Brady nodded her agreement and approached the hostess. "Hi we have a reservation for seven thirty."

"Donner party of seven?"

"Yes. Donner Party." Brady nodded. "And boy are we hungry." Immediately her face crinkled up and she giggled like a schoolgirl.

Ralph laughed as well.

After snorting, Brady caught her laughter and waved out her hand to the hostess. "Sorry, even after twenty years, that still makes me laugh."

The hostess tilted her head in question.

Brady explained, "Donner party. Hungry?"

The hostess was still clueless.

"Oh, well, look it up, you'll laugh later."

The hostess passed on an awkward smile, grabbed menus and led the way.

Brady still giggled, despite Bobby nudging her to quit.

It wasn't as if Cyrus was always late, but Opus acted like it. He had no tolerance for anyone's tardiness. Brady attributed that to his 'General Manager' status at a coffeehouse franchise. Opus was the serious one. More serious than Cyrus, who had every reason to be serious. Perseus was too young to be so serious, Bobby often didn't get why things were serious, but to Opus … everything was. Brady knew him since he was just a Java Joe coffee boy who worked his way up the corporate ladder. Even though he had low tolerance. He was that anal coffee boy that always suggested to the manager on which employee could do a better job.

Opus looked at his watch every five seconds, as if that would make Cyrus arrive faster.

Finally, after only ten minutes late, Cyrus sent a text to go on and order appetizers, he would be there in a few. He had been delayed at the car-rental place.

Ralph did his typical asking of the waitress, 'odd or even', and when she said 'even', he told her he wanted to order every other appetizer, in order, starting with the second.

Cyrus showed up just as the appetizers were placed on the table. He said, "Perfect timing," passed a round of kisses to everyone and ordered a triple Jack Daniels, straight with a straw, before he even placed his bottom in a chair.

"Long week," Cyrus said, inching his chair toward the table.

No two Donner men looked or acted alike. Bobby had the peppered hair with the blue-collar look and demeanor. Perseus was still young, gawky and thin, almost shy at times. Opus was all business and the only ginger and balding man in the family. Cyrus was a throwback who didn't worry much about his appearance; when his light brown hair grew a little long in the front, he didn't think twice about pulling it back in a woman's headband or using his glasses to keep it from his eyes.

Truth be known, Cyrus had better things to do with this time.

"Got a gift," Ralph announced, as those around the table plated the shrimp appetizers. "Not much, but a new product."

He then proceeded to open a bag and pass out the rectangular, tin, meat-product cans to everyone. "New flavors. You guys get to try them first during the test run."

Brady was ecstatic. "Oh, wow, Teriyaki."

"Yep." Ralph nodded and passed a can. "Buffalo. Sweet and Sour, and my personal new test favorite … Jamaican Jerk."

Opus lifted his can and gave a look of 'falsely' being impressed. "Jamaican Jerk Spam."

"No, no. I don't make Spam." Ralph waved a finger. "Not Spam. Never Spam. Canned Meat product."

Opus nodded. "Well, at least it'll be favorable in the apocalypse for us."

At first, Cyrus choked. "Sorry." He hit his own chest and then took a big gulp of his drink. "Speaking of the apocalypse."

Opus curled his lip. "No one was speaking of the apocalypse, I was making a joke."

"Yes, well, it's a great segue for what I have to say. First …" He reached for a roll and grabbed his knife, peering at Brady. "I really would like you not to put Samantha in school this year."

Brady chuckled. "She's three. Who puts their three-year-old in school?"

"Everyone," Cyrus said.

"Well, then I'm behind on the parent eight ball. That's just wrong; I mean, she'd be in school twenty years. Why am I not wanting her in school?"

"Things are happening, they aren't good." Cyrus looked up from the buttering of his roll.

Ralph exhaled. "Oh, boy. Knowing where you work, this isn't good."

Bobby winced. "Cyrus, come on. Really? Right now? You think this is time to scare everyone."

"Yeah it is, Bob," Cyrus retorted. "Cause as my family you guys need to be aware. What if you weren't and come Tuesday when things come out, you'll be like 'Cyrus why didn't you tell us.'"

Opus shook his head. "No we wouldn't."

"Yes, you would," Cyrus continued. "You especially, Op. I just need you guys to be prepared. This isn't good. This is bigger than everyone knows and it'll get worse. I'm meeting with a presidential committee shortly. I'm hoping to have my findings together by then. I'll let you guys know first."

Bobby asked, "What does this have to do with?"

"Children."

Bobby nodded. "The candy."

"That's a cover story until it's broken. Now … this thing is old, decades old. So we have some history to base it on, but it's changed. It doesn't affect any child younger than five." Cyrus looked at Brady. "Which gives me two years to fix it. I will. And it doesn't affect anyone over fifteen." He looked at Perseus. "Unless you get bit, or scratched, or spit on. Then it's lethal immediately and that's where our concern lies."

"What animal?" Ralph asked. "What will bite us?"

"Children," Cyrus replied almost nonchalantly, then smiled when the waitress set down his plate. "Ah, dinner. I'm starved. Thanks."

71

He may have dove directly into his food, but before they could eat, the others at the table were still digesting his words.

NODDING – JACQUELINE DRUGA

Chapter Ten

Pittsburgh, PA

"Gio was killed, how did this happen?" his mother sobbed. "How did he die? What happened?"

Nola didn't have the answers, she cried right along with his mother, Murielle. Giovanni was a great kid. He was absolutely fine before he turned into some sort of madman. He hit against Nola's door until he killed himself.

By the time the police had arrived, Gio had died.

They took Carlie immediately to the local hospital's emergency room, and then transported her down to Pittsburgh to Children's Hospital. They brought Gio there as well.

Pushing midnight, Nola was concerned about her boys being home. Even though the neighbor was keeping an eye out, she was worried.

She was placed in a waiting room different than where every other parent waited. So there was no denying that the doctor was there to speak to her when he walked in the room.

"Mrs. Carson."

Nola released Murielle's hand and stood. "Yes. How's my daughter?"

"She's fine. She's resting. She'll heal just fine from the injury."

Nola nodded. Carlie had been bleeding from where her hair was pulled. "Will it grow back?"

"It should."

"So I can take her home?"

The doctor shook his head. "No, we need to keep her here a few days to watch."

"Watch for what?" Nola asked. "Is this more than you're telling me? Did she have a head injury?"

"We are watching for signs of exposure."

Nola stepped back. "Exposure. You think she ate that candy?"

"We don't know."

Murielle stood. "But my son didn't. I'm sure of it. I didn't buy any."

The doctor looked at Gio's mom. "We can't go by the assumption that a child didn't consume something just because the parent didn't buy it. Children eat candy, they share. So we're watching."

"Can I see her?" Nola asked.

"Not right now. In a little while we'll bring you to her room. If you'll excuse me …" The doctor turned.

"No," Nola said. "I'm not going to excuse you or this vague bedside manner. Run a test, check her blood. Something."

The doctor partially shrugged. "It's not that easy. I will tell you if nothing shows in a few days then she can go. I have several children here we are trying to subdue and—"

"Several? Nola questioned. "Like Gio."

"Excuse me." He didn't hesitate, the doctor just left the small room.

Nola threw out her hands. "What the hell am I supposed to do?" After saying those words, Nola realized that her troubles were minimal compared to what Murielle was going through. "I'm so sorry. I am sorry, that was insensitive of me."

Murielle shook her head. "I know my son didn't eat that candy. I know he didn't."

"I believe you. But what else could have caused it?"

"Virus maybe. Seizures."

Nola exhaled heavily; it was going to be a long night, possibly even a long couple days. She worried. A few minutes earlier she was just concerned that Carlie's injury would be all right, now she feared that Carlie consumed that candy, or worse, like Murielle suggested, exposed to a virus. At wits' end, Nola didn't know where else to turn, so she did what she had been avoiding doing all night. She picked up the phone and called her brother. It rang and he answered. "Hello, Tom. Hey, it's me. I have a problem."

New York, NY

Tom hadn't been sleeping and despite how quiet he tried to be, Jill was awake. She sat up in bed as Tom returned to the room. They had a nice sized bedroom, Tom's computer was in the corner by the window and he walked over to pour a drink.

"Tom? Everything okay?"

"That was Nola. Apparently ..." Tom paused to down the drink. "That incident in Pittsburgh involved my sister. Carlie was attacked by the boy and is in the hospital right now under observation. More like quarantine. Nola knows it isn't right. She's not buying the candy story but what can she do. They aren't telling her anything."

"Wait." Jill tossed off the covers and stood. "That was in a trailer park. Nola doesn't live in a trailer park. She has that house. I know it's been a while ..."

"It's been too long, Jill." Tom exhaled. "She comes here to visit. We never go there. Should have known by that damn beat-up fucking van." Tom tossed out his hands.

"How is Carlie?"

"They said she's fine. But they're watching her. The kid ripped out her hair."

"Nola?"

"Handling. I'm sick." Tom closed his eyes. "It was my family. My family that was involved and I didn't even know because my own sister felt too ashamed to tell me how bad things have been. She lost the house. I covered this attack like a newsman."

"You can't blame yourself. Nola is a proud woman. You've helped her in the past and she hated every time she had to ask you." Jill laid her hand on Tom's shoulder. "Can you take time to go down there? It is the holiday weekend."

"Would you mind?" Tom asked. "With Carlie in the hospital under quarantine, the boys are with a neighbor. I'd like to go and help her out."

"I'll go into the account and see if we can get you a flight." Jill stepped back.

"I hate leaving you and the kids."

"Me, Jen, and Jerrod will be just fine. Besides, no outbreaks here. I'd rather keep it that way."

Before Jill sat down at Tom's computer, he grabbed her, embraced her and then kissed her. "I love you, you know that. You're amazing."

Jill just smiled. "You have a lot on your mind. It's a been an awful couple weeks for you."

"And it's only gonna get worse."

She gave him a look of sympathy.

Tom exhaled heavily, and then lifted his phone.

"Are you calling Nola to tell her you're coming?"

"In a second, right now ... I'm calling Cyrus. If anyone can help out, get answers, it's him. After all, this is his project now." Tom began to dial. He was grateful for his new friend in a high place. Tom felt queasy and his head started to hurt. Jill was right, he did have a couple of bad weeks, but the outbreak, mystery illness, it still wasn't real to him until that very moment when it took on a new perspective. It didn't just hit close to home, it affected his family.

Ripley, WV

Perseus didn't talk much; he was shy by nature and became more of an introvert when his parents died a few years earlier. But that wasn't the reason he didn't talk. It was choice. Even as a child he didn't talk and when he did it wasn't much.

When he wasn't speaking at all and only pointing to things at the age of three, his parents sought help. They stopped believing that Perseus was going to be like Einstein and speak when he had something to say.

That wasn't the case.

He just didn't want to talk.

He attended speech and spoke fine to the therapist in the back room but reverted back into silence after leaving.

By the time he was six he was speaking a lot. Being the youngest, his voice was buried. One on one Perseus was a cool kid to talk to.

He wanted to talk to Cyrus. Just as they relaxed on the porch alone, Cyrus took a call.

Perseus waited.

"Everything all right?" Perseus asked, when Cyrus returned.

"Yes, a friend of mine. He needed a favor, but I was headed there tomorrow anyhow."

"You really have to leave?"

Cyrus sat down next to Perseus. "I really do. This is gonna get pretty big."

"How is that possible?"

"A few factors. Mostly it's theories I am working on and I have only a few days to substantiate those theories."

"Does what happened in Le Roy, New York, a few years ago, have anything to do with this?"

Cyrus smiled. "Wow, I am so impressed with you knowing about the buried epidemics."

Perseus shrugged. "You're my brother; I am always keeping up on the CDC website."

"Good boy." Cyrus patted his brother's knee. "No. Doubtful. Maybe from the same family of virus. Those kids really didn't hurt anyone but themselves and ... they have a tic here and there, but they're alive."

"Meaning the kids that get this will die?"

"If they aren't killed in the process or kill themselves, they won't live, no."

"Aw man, aw man, that's sad." Perseus shook his head. "You got to work on this thing. You have to do it for Sammy."

"I know, I will."

"Are ... are you sacred about how big this is gonna get?"

"Yes," Cyrus said assuredly, then moistened his lips and faced Perseus. "But I'm more scared of what people will do when they know how big it can get. That ... that is what scares me more."

Chapter Eleven

September 6

Pittsburgh, PA

Tom remembered the days when Children's Hospital of Pittsburgh was more accessible to driving and not so much a 'chain-style' medical center. They seemed to handle everything like a proficient assembly line at a factory. He wished they thought of location when building the new place. Traffic was a headache and there weren't any hotels nearby.

The closest was a couple miles away and he guessed that was better for Nola than traveling 30 miles from her home.

He managed to park, and the emergency room had been sectioned off. He tried to get answers about his niece but was unable to. While there, he saw three children coming in, secured with restraints and thrashing.

Three more.

He tried to call Cyrus, but it went straight to voice mail. He guessed he was en route. Unable to get by the security desk, Tom finally got a hold of Nola. She came down to the lobby, exhausted, worn, and she raced right into her big brother's arms.

Immediately, she cried.

Tom folded. He couldn't recall Nola shedding a tear since the day Eddie was hit by the car. She showed only strength when her husband died.

"It'll be okay," Tom told her. That was all he had to offer.

"No, it won't. They only let me see her through a window. Tom, she's crying. She doesn't understand."

"Look." He pulled her from him and looked at her. "I have a friend with the CDC; he's on his way here. We'll get some answers, okay?"

Nola nodded.

"Let's go to your place, get the boys and bring them to the hotel."

"Hotel?" Nola tilted her head. "Tom, you can stay with me."

"I know, but that's a far jaunt for you, Nola, the hotel is closer. Would you like to go there and I'll go get the boys?"

"No, I need to see them. But I'm glad you drove. I rode here with the ambulance."

"Then let's go." Tom placed his arm around her and led her from the lobby.

Nola expressed she was hungry, but declined when Tom offered to stop for food. She didn't say much, just stared out the window, and a third of the way to Mon City, Nola fell asleep.

Tom hated to wake her, but he didn't know where she lived. He only knew how to get to the town.

When Tom was given the address of New Eagle Mobile Homes Estates, he really expected an estate like the one in Lancaster. Lots well maintained, a community center, fenced in area, and all the mobile homes in good, attractive condition. Admittedly, he didn't watch the news report, only read it. It was disturbing, so he didn't watch it, if he had, he wouldn't have been so surprised.

What was his sister thinking? The place had to be so affordable and her situation so dire that she had no other choice.

His first thought was a refugee camp. The mobile homes were more like trailers and crammed together like a slum. The road was gravel and most of the mobile homes were so old and falling apart, they were on the verge of being condemned.

Tom was obviously a social-class bigot because the folks who lived there looked absolutely nothing like he imagined.

They weren't lazy, unbathed people, sitting on folding chairs drinking beer.

He saw a mechanic, a woman wearing nurse's scrubs. These were people down on their luck, making the best of the situation, maybe trying to get back on their feet.

Nola's trailer wasn't too bad, older, but it had a porch with a wheelchair ramp. Her van was right out front. But there was one thing Tom noticed that he didn't see … children.

There were no children. It was Saturday afternoon, where were they?

As Tom stepped from the rented van he saw the blood on the door frame of Nola's home and the police tape dangled.

Nola whispered out, "Gio."

Tom reached over placing a hand on her shoulder. "Not many children in this community."

Nola stopped walking at the base of her ramp. "There are a ton. They play over …" She pointed to the right of her trailer. A beat-up swing set and slide were there and not a soul was around. "Something is up. It's too quiet." She turned left to right. "Where are they?"

A squeak then slam of a metal screen porch door rang out before a woman called, "Nola."

Tom turned and so did Nola.

"Sharon." Nola exhaled.

"Nola? What …" Sharon tilted her head. "What are you doing here?"

"I came home to clean up. They wouldn't let me see Carlie. And I wanted to see the boys. This is my brother, Tom."

It wasn't rudeness that caused Sharon to ignore Tom's extended hand, it was her focus on Nola.

"What is it?" Nola asked. "What's wrong?"

"I thought you'd be with the other parents. I came home from work and … they took the kids, Nola. They took all the kids four and older, to quarantine."

Tom felt the shocking blow; he could only imagine what Nola felt. But she was cool, calm, and focused.

"Do you know where?" Nola asked.

Sharon shook her head. "I don't have children so I don't know. It was done when I got back."

Nola exhaled with sadness.

81

"Don't worry," Tom told her. "I'll call my friend as soon as he lands. He's flying in."

Nola acknowledged with a nod, then told Sharon, "Thank you," squeezed her hand then walked toward the trailer.

"Keep me posted. Let me know what's going on," Sharon spoke as they walked from her.

At the door, Nola paused.

"What is it?" Tom asked.

"Video game," Nola whispered, grabbed her key, unlocked the door and barged in.

She squealed out an 'oh'.

Tom hurried in behind her and saw why she was delighted. Eddie was in front of the television.

"Mom? Uncle Tom?" Eddie put down the controller and turned his motorized chair.

"Eddie," Nola gasped out, and ran to him. "I thought they took you. I thought they took all the kids. Sharon said they did."

Eddie nodded. "They did, mom. I heard them coming. You know how I hear real good."

Tom reached down and grabbed Eddie's arm. "Do you know where they took the kids?"

"No." Eddie shook his head. "I heard them knocking next door. I heard them saying they were taking all the kids between the ages of four and fifteen. People were screaming and fighting."

Nola asked, "Why didn't they take you?"

"I lied. They asked my age and I said I was sixteen. I also said I wasn't outside."

Nola smiled. "That was smart. That was really smart. But we still have to find your brother."

Eddie dropped his voice to a whisper, "He's hiding. He's in your closet. I told him to hide. He did. You aren't mad are you?"

"Oh my God, no. No." Nola kissed Eddie. "I'm not mad at you at all. You are so smart, so, so smart."

"I didn't want them to take him. So when they said they knew there was a boy here, I said he went with an aunt because I couldn't watch him."

"Amazing thinking, Eddie. I'm proud of you." Tom laid his hand on Eddie's head then kissed him.

Nola, who had been crouching, stood and walked to the hall. Tom followed behind. In a determined stride, Nola walked straight into her room and opened her closet.

Ben gasped and jumped a little, covered his mouth. He slid down his hand, smiled widely and jumped into his mother's arms.

"I'm so glad you're here."

Ben whispered, "I'm being quiet. I don't want anyone to know I'm here."

"You're okay. I have you. I have you now." Nola held tight, then glanced up to Tom. "Why are they taking all the kids? They weren't around Gio."

Tom shook his head. "I don't know. But I'll find out."

Tom would. He also knew, for the time being, until he received some answers, it was best to keep Ben hidden, for how long, remained to be seen.

Ripley, WV

Brady could smell breakfast, long before she even finished walking down the stairs. Sammy wasn't in her bed, and Brady didn't have to guess where she was. Sammy was with Ralph.

In fact, no one was sleeping. She heard a barrage of male voices flowing from the kitchen, intermittently laced with little-girl giggles.

"Morning." Ralph smiled, walked over to Brady and kissed her on the cheek. "The baby ate three pieces of the Maple Bacon Morning flavor."

Brady headed for the coffee. "You didn't announce that flavor at dinner."

Ralph winked. "It was a surprise."

Perseus held up his fork. "It tastes just like bacon."

"Held the fat, half the time," Ralph said. "Opus?"

"I love it."

After running her hand over Bobby's head, Brady took a seat next to him. "Where's Cyrus?"

Bobby replied, "He had to leave. There was an emergency in Pittsburgh."

"Pittsburgh is close," Brady said.

"We're good," Bobby replied. "Remember? Two years."

"Can't count on that." Ralph joined them at the table. "Hey there, Perse, can you take the baby into the other room. Cartoons are on. I wanna update Brady here on what's going on."

"Sure thing, Ralph." Perseus stood, walked to the booster chair, and after lifting a plate, he lifted Sammy. "Come on, Sam. Let's watch TV."

Brady tried to read their faces. Ralph, who was usually jovial, looked concerned. Opus, as always, was serious, and Bobby seemed to not care.

"What's going on?" Brady asked.

"Cyrus left," Ralph answered. "Seems there's now a dozen or so kids in Pittsburgh with this thing. What concerns me, is what Opus saw on the Internet. Tell her."

Phone in hand, Opus handed his device to Brady. "Pittsburgh and a neighboring county went into quarantine, they are dismissing what the CDC is saying and overruling their suggestions. They started quarantining any and all children between the ages of four and fifteen that have been in contact or in a radius of the infected in a several day span. The one

84

newscaster said they're talking student bodies of ten different schools."

"What does Cyrus say?" Brady asked.

"Well, I called him," Opus replied. "He was unaware of this but said he'd let us know as soon as he landed. He should be there now."

"Can they do this?" Brady asked. "Can Pittsburgh do this?"

Ralph nodded. "Boston locked down a city of a million, over one mad and injured bomber. Enraged and rabid kids … yeah, they can. Which got me to thinking and Opus agrees. One city doing it, means every city doing it."

Opus added, "They're gonna lock healthy kids in with infected kids and what will you get? Every kid infected."

"What can we do?" Brady asked.

Bobby answered, "Nothing."

"No." Ralph shook his head. "I'm gonna start prepping a hideaway. A sanctuary that you and Sammy can run to. Hidden, safe, stocked, until this thing blows over. We keep an eye on the situation and when it starts to really bubble. You go. No waiting. You go with the baby."

"This is scaring me," Brady said.

"It should. Be scared." Ralph laid his hand on hers. "Being scared will get you ready."

"It's ridiculous," Bobby stated strongly. "This …" He motioned his hand out to the table. "It's overboard. Really. Running? Hiding?" He huffed out a breath and stood. "It's not necessary and it won't touch us."

Opus asked, "How can you be so sure?"

"We have two years." Bobby walked to the coffee pot. "Won't touch us, why worry."

"Bobby," Brady spoke passionately. "How are you so indifferent about this?"

"Because, Brady, Cyrus is on this. If anyone can stop this, he can. I trust him. I believe in him, and maybe now …" He poured a cup of coffee. "So should all of you. And instead of wasting time plotting a hideaway, spend the time with person that you want to hide. Like I am, right now." He put down the pot and walked from the kitchen.

For as much as Brady herself believed in Cyrus, he was only one man. Even one man with an answer could get lost in a sea of angry and scared people.

Every virus or illness has a reference name. Not an official medical name like H5N1, but rather like, Bird Flu, Spanish Flu, Small Pox, SARS.

Cyrus came up with his name for the new bug while watching a few of the infected while in quarantine.

Of the twelve infected who remained alive, two were sleeping the rest unaffected by the sedatives or anticonvulsive medications that had worked on similar occasions.

The ones not responding to medication were restrained, yet maddened and focused on freeing themselves.

Watching them freak-out, Cyrus thought of Sammy when she didn't get her way. Out of control. Because of that, he called the germ ... Tantrum.

Three more had been confirmed infected in the Allegheny and Washington County areas of Pennsylvania. But they died in the midst of their attacks. All under the age of eight.

The twelve were placed there in psychiatric observation rooms. Little clothing, no furniture, more like caged animals in a padded cell and it was for their protection.

Tom Gibson's niece was in a general quarantine room, she had been injured and Cyrus ordered a specimen from her immediately. A fresh one, he wanted to see if he could 'see' it.

He'd keep Tom posted on all of it.

Cyrus was certain in a few days that number of twelve was going to be a hundred. Maybe even more. Unless, of course, the quarantine was allowed to remain in effect. Then that number would be higher.

While Cyrus saw the reasoning for the Mayor's executive decision, he couldn't condone it. Five deaths, outside the attacks, just individuals who may have been exposed to infected saliva or blood, they were dead. That was the Mayor's reason.

It didn't take a rocket scientist to realize, infected candy didn't cause that. Plus, the Health Department Director commented on the fact that Razzle was an expensive candy, most of the infected with Tantrum weren't going to buy that candy.

On his advice, and suspicions that counteracted with what Cyrus put out there as the CDC, the Mayor granted the quarantine.

It wasn't just for the protection of the children; it was for those around them.

Within two hours of Pittsburgh announcing its youth safety quarantine, Philadelphia, Boston, and Alexandria did the same.

It was insane, Cyrus knew it.

They packed the kids into schools and awaited Red Cross blankets and food.

It reminded Cyrus of the forties and the concentration camps. It wasn't right, it wasn't fair, and they were children. Children who were scared and didn't do anything wrong.

He observed how much of a madhouse Pittsburgh became. Parents were angry, mobbing outside the schools.

Screaming for their children back.

Cyrus was trying, he really was trying. So was the President for that matter. Even though the constitution prohibited the federal government from intervening, the President still went into emergency session to create an executive order banning state quarantines in the interest of the general population.

Time would tell if it would work. Though, the longer it took, the worse it would be for cities that huddled children together.

The best defense against the spread was to keep children in their homes, because putting them all together in one building wasn't preventing the spread—it was creating a breeding ground.

District 3

Three Months Post-Detaining

In the beginning, it was insane. Once people found out where the Detaining Districts were being built, not just thousands, but *tens* of thousands rushed to the redesigned cities.

The woman was one of the first of hundreds to arrive. A military blockade, larger than she could imagine, created a perimeter miles outside of The District and all around it. They built a blockade a mile before the military perimeter. Keeping people at a distance and keeping them in the dark as to what was going on. Once she got there, there was no turning back. She physically couldn't unless she walked, but she was already hundreds of miles from home.

What was most important in the world, was beyond that military barricade.

She had supplies; she just had to hold out hope. It was a mistake, that was what she first thought. A huge mistake and soon it would be rectified. Someone out there would put a stop to it.

But they didn't. They couldn't.

Their reasoning was, if the human race was to survive and continue—it had to be done.

Not in her book, there were answers.

In the first month after the Detaining, people came to the barricade. She was front lines, yet she couldn't see beyond the walls of a tunnel and didn't hear anything but construction noise. Loud noise, all day, all night. When she stepped from the tunnel for air, she could see the glow of the lights reflecting off the sky.

What were they doing?

At first, people waited. As if, when they took down the barricade, they'd be able to get in. People tried. The woman heard rumors of people jumping into the river, trying to swim—taking boats, all of the attempts in vain and ending tragically.

No one got in. No one got out.

People had nothing else to do. Most stopped working a month before the Detaining rule. They couldn't work, taking care of the infected prohibited that. And because no one left their homes, society was a mess. Things shut down—utilities, business, hospitals, and eventually the economy.

Globally, it was the same. Life came to a halt. Cities went dark.

Then the Detaining and Cleansing went into effect. Renewal Cities were announced; cities with lights, power, medical provisions, and food.

No one cared at first, then after a month, after the Detaining and Cleansing took what it could, people did care. The woman saw this. People left their cars and belongings and left the barricade. She supposed they headed to the Renewal Cities. Put the past behind, start anew.

Not her. She couldn't.

She wouldn't.

Three days before the barricades went down, the construction noise stopped. It was quiet. The woman knew whatever they were building, had been done.

The next day there were explosions, tympanic booms filled the air, leaving dark clouds in the sky.

Then finally, the barricade lifted. The woman didn't know this, no one did. It wasn't announced. She and a thousand or so others were in and outside a tunnel. A tunnel that led to the city being renamed as District 3.

The tunnel was blocked halfway through. Roads going to the large hill that ran south of the city were blocked and destroyed. District 3 was a mystery until that day.

A man who grew tired of waiting, a man who knew the silence meant something, broke through the barricade, saying he had nothing to lose and didn't care if he was shot.

He returned and announced the military was gone.

At first, people didn't rush, at least the first group right there with the woman at the beginning. They moved cautiously in droves through the blockade and emerged on the other side of the tunnel. A tunnel that once led to a bridge. That bridge was gone.

The woman was rendered breathless. All bridges leading into the city had been destroyed and the city, shrouded by a cloud of debris, was surrounded by a concrete wall. District 3 was a horrific prison of some sorts.

Immediately she backed up and stayed with her back against the wall of the tunnel.

She had a keen foresight, and she was correct. There was nowhere to go but down. There was no wall. No blockade, just an end to a bridge and the river below. The more people that came from the tunnel, the closer to the edge the crowd grew. Suddenly they charged from the tunnel pushing into the ones that had stopped.

It was a matter of seconds.

The woman watched.

And just as she feared, the anger, anticipation, and anxiousness of the crowd pushed forward, sending multitudes of people over the edge into the water and riverbank below.

People screamed. They shoved. They fell. The woman witnessed in horror as hundreds fell to their death. Arms flailing as they tried to purchase a hold on the air and failed, dropping down. Some hitting the river, some hitting the concrete wharf below. Thud, thud, splash, splash. Thud splash.

She stayed put, away from the masses.

Falling to her death into the river was not an option, getting close to the wall of District 3 was. And for that, she had to plan.

PART THREE: RED ROVER, RED ROVER

Curse of the Innocents

September 14

Po Toi O, Sai Kung, New Territories, Hong Kong

His village was small and set in the Clearwater Bay Peninsula, modest homes, but he needed very little. Shelter, food, and clothing for his family.

He was a simple man, a fisherman, who made his living off of what he caught. He considered himself very fortunate because the fish were drawn to him. The night before he studied the sky and knew the next day would bring much. With it being a Sunday, there would be very few men on the water.

The days of the week didn't dictate when he would work.

Sky still dark in the early morning, he stepped outside to take in the peacefulness and think before venturing out on his boat. It was immediately as he stepped out that the stench caught him.

It was horrendous and overwhelming, and it carried in the wind from the direction of the bay. He stepped from his home, down the path and to the pier. As he did so, he saw it.

The moon was still in the sky, lighting the area and the beams of the moon cast upon objects floating in the bay.

Many objects.

The man was horrified, instantly believing that something had contaminated the water and all the fish had died. He raced back to his home to grab his spotlight and when in the house, he noticed the empty sleeping mat.

Where were his children? An immediate sense of panic struck him and he hurried to his sleeping wife. Just as his hand touched upon her shoulder, a cry cut through the silence of the village.

A deep, agonizing cry that repeated.

His wife stirred abruptly from her sleep and asked what was happening. He didn't answer, and a foreboding feeling swam in his gut. Spotlight in hand, he raced outside. Soon the one voice screaming became two and three, and he heard the splashing of water.

Were people jumping in the bay?

The pier wasn't far, and he flicked on the light as he hit the wooden planks. More cries, more screams rang out and the man focused the beam of his light on the water.

Villagers ran into the bay, arms flailing, crying out names, and that was when the man saw. It wasn't fish floating in the water—it was the bodies of children.

Many children.

Most of the children from the village.

They floated stomachs down, their dark hair masqueraded their heads within the water and the whites of their flesh reflected off of the moon, making their small carcasses look like floating fish.

He was certain his children were there. He put down the light, and like the others, jumped in the water.

The man didn't know how they ended up there. He, like the others, believed someone snuck into their homes and did this. But the truth was, while the man slept, his children, like many others, were overcome with Tantrum. They simply woke, were in a nonviolent episode and not knowing what they did or why, every child over the age of five, walked into the bay. They didn't swim or make a noise. They just drowned.

Chapter Twelve

September 15

Washington, DC

President Henry Collingsworth placed his daughter in the car and sent her off to school, and as he stood in the meeting room just outside of the Oval Office, he wished he hadn't.

He recalled the conversation that morning with his wife, Maria.

"She's not going," Maria argued. "I want her here."

"She has to go. We are urging people to keep normal routines."

"But it's everywhere, Henry. Everywhere."

"It's not here."

"Yet, or we just don't know."

"Maria ..." he sighed out. "If I keep her home, it shows the American people I do no practice what I preach. It shows I am scared. What kind of message am I sending."

"A wise one. Keep the children away from others," her words were passionate, strong.

Henry didn't listen, he couldn't.

Now he stood before a line of televisions, reporting that hospitals in China were filing up, and health officials were at a loss at what to do. The stock market opened disastrously and was falling by the second. Half of the American work force didn't go to work. Hiding out.

"How did it get to this?" The young President ran his hand down his unshaven face. "How did it explode so quickly?"

His Chief Health Advisor, John Alberts, spoke with frustration, "It didn't explode; it just ... came to a head."

"Not yet," the voice entered the room, it was Cyrus Donner. "Not yet. This is not a head."

"Cyrus," Alberts sighed out. "Thank you for coming."

"That big guy let me in." He dropped a folder on the table.

The President pointed to the folder. "That looks like an awfully small folder for a big situation."

"Oh, there's more. But what I need to say, mostly, is here." Cyrus pointed to his head. "And it's not a lot to remember, because this thing is an anomaly of nature. I have some facts, some theories, and that's more than anyone else."

Alberts nodded. "I've read what Cyrus has and what I have. We're on the same lines."

After peering at the televisions once more, the President sat down. "What are we looking at, Dr. Donner? How did this thing come out of nowhere?"

"Well, it didn't," Cyrus explained. "It's been around for decades. Just not everywhere. It's been on a slow spread throughout the Uganda and Tanzania regions. When it first occurred, everyone blamed a chemical weapon. But ... that wouldn't cause new cases yearly."

Alberts added, "It is known as the Nodding Disease. Given that name because the victim will nod, as if falling asleep before each episode."

Cyrus said, "These episodes, like the Nodding, have evolved. At first they were more like seizures, causing the children to just stare and be drone like. Then, through the years, the episodes became violent. Those infected had rage episodes where they attacked. Parents tied up their children. But the children chewed through the restraints. They feel no pain, no emotion, and don't recall. Much like our children now, they cycle. Calm, drone, lucid, violent."

The President asked, "If this has been around for decades why haven't we found a cure?"

Cyrus shook his head. "Ignorance, location. Arrogance. We thought it could be controlled by anti-seizure medications, and it was low priority for seeking a cure because of its isolated region. But as it evolved, it was less responsive to any treatment. See,

96

we should have looked at the big picture instead of the region. Seventy to a hundred percent of children between the ages of five and fifteen got this. In all regions. The disease stunts growth, mentality, and the child succumbs in three to seven years. We never looked at the region as a possible global scenario."

"Do we know what it is? What causes it?" the President asked.

Cyrus nodded. "I have good idea. At first it was believed to be a microscopic parasite or nematode because a parasite was found in seventy percent of all victims. But why not all? It can't be the parasite if all the victims don't have it. So, my guess, nematodes are living organisms with digestive tracts, and I think it's the digestive waste of the nematode causing a reactive bacterial infection that is highly contagious. In children, the infection causes the Nodding, or Tantrum as we call it. It has a three to five day incubation in children and a five to ten minute reaction in adults. The bacteria is deadly to any adult exposed to it. It's not airborne, but it's microscopic and it's easily transmitted."

"Jesus." The President ran his hand down his face. "Wait. Bacteria. Can't we fight that with antibiotics?"

Alberts answered, "We're trying. But it's resistant with the children, and as far as adults go, it hits so rapidly no antibiotic can work that fast."

Cyrus explained, "Using chicken pox as a bad analogy ... chicken pox affects kids differently than adults, this does too."

"How did it spread so fast?" the President asked.

"It was contained for a while in its remote area," Cyrus answered. "But it got out. A fly on a person, bug, you name it. That's all it took. Insects carry this thing. It lives on surfaces, through blood, saliva. So it can be left anywhere. When SARS hit, a cockroach carried it through an apartment complex, infecting a thousand people. We have the same thing happening here. The nematode catches a ride on a bug, a kid gets it. He spreads the bacteria. We just came out of summer, that's how it got out of control so fast. And it's faster. It's nowhere near reaching the head. Three weeks ago, we had six reported incidents. Two weeks ago, seventy-two, last week it was in the high hundreds, this week, thousands. Next week is a nightmare. We don't have health care facilities to handle it or treatments. It's off the map."

"What do we do?" President Collingsworth questioned.

Alberts answered, "We cure or inhibit it. Create a cure for the kids to stop spreading it and an inhibitor for adults, like a vaccine, but we're looking realistically, if we come up with the magical answer today, it will be a year until we can distribute the cure or inhibitor."

Cyrus exhaled. "We have to stop it at the source. We can't find every bug, toy, candy, that has it. We have to focus on the children. They are the breeders and spreaders. Because a year at this rate of infection—is extinction."

The President's eyes widened. "Surely you're exaggerating, Dr. Donner."

Cyrus shook his head. "I wish I was. Now, things do mysterious stop as fast as they start. This could very well end tomorrow with no more infections. I doubt it though. You see, nature has a way of fixing mistakes. Humans haven't been around that long. What if we as humans are the mistake? We are destroying this planet. We know it. This could possibly be nature's control switch. What better way to do it, eliminate the species by eliminating the future. If this bacteria hits every child, in ten years we aren't looking at a world controlled by outraged children. We're looking at a dead world. All the children infected will die; all the adults around them … will die."

"We need a plan and one fast, while we work on that cure," Alberts said.

"If securing the future starts with the infected children," the President slowly stood, his face drawn with worry, "then maybe, as harsh as this sounds, we secure that future by securing those children." He coughed out what could only be a holding back of emotion, excused himself and left the room.

Mon City, PA

It was the first, and it was going to be far from the last, time Nola saw the 'No Children Allowed' sign. They were becoming commonplace over the last several days as news of the outbreaks increased.

No children at gas stations.

No children at restaurants.

No children … at hotels.

Almost every store up and down Main Street had a handwritten sign in the window. It wasn't even illegal because no one cared.

Nola did because she had nowhere to go. Her mobile home court was quarantined, shut down, because three days after Gio took ill, six other children who weren't even playing with him, came down with Tantrum.

Not to mention, Ringgold Elementary was closed. It opened for the first week of school after Labor Day and announced on Friday that it would remain closed indefinitely. All the children, except Nola's that was, had been gathered and placed there for that short quarantine time. But not long after they were released, they started falling ill.

Almost as if the argument that it was a breeding ground was true.

Perhaps that was why Carlie and Ben weren't sick. Eddie was pushing the age limits and Nola didn't worry quite so much about him getting sick. She worried more about being around someone that was. Eddie was defenseless to an attack.

The children changed almost instantaneously once Tantrum took effect. They stared for a few seconds, then nodded, then went rabid.

She hated leaving Eddie alone with Ben and Carlie for the simple fear that, God Forbid, they turned, Eddie couldn't do anything. So asking them to understand and forgive her, Nola made homemade restraints that gave Carlie and Ben ability to move, but not get too close to Eddie. She hated to do it, hated to leave, but she had to. Nola needed a place to live; she had very little money and couldn't drive around all day. She thought about camping, going to the mountains and waiting for the infection to wither out. Mr. Melbourne was kind enough to let Nola and the kids stay in the back of the Laundromat. Only for a short time. He announced that if things didn't change in a week, he'd have to close.

She couldn't stay with Tom, considering her children were in an infected area, she didn't want to take that chance.

After putting a few dollars of gas in the van, she drove to the nearby town of Donora; there was small roadside motel that was pretty run down.

It was dirty, but in Nola's eyes it was a roof over their heads and probably affordable.

When motel guy told them the weekly room rates, Nola had enough to rent for two weeks. She felt relieved until he asked, "Do you have any children? No kids allowed. Not right now."

Nola wanted to break, fold, and cry. In fact she did. As she turned to leave, the motel owner must have felt bad.

"You're not the only one. Apartment buildings have been quarantined. Lots of families displaced," he said. "I feel bad, I can't help you. But, if you turn on KDKA radio, they've been announcing places that are taking families. Last one I heard was a KOA campsite just outside of Washington, PA, that's taking families. You can try there. They may be full. Also some outside of Claysville."

100

Claysville, Washington, while not that far, would be a big distance to drive to work. Then again, how much longer would Nola have a job?

She thanked him and got back in her van.

Following his advice, she immediately put on the radio station.

In the short drive back to work, she heard a lot of sentiments that reflected the ones going through her mind.

Callers dialing in.

When are we gonna hear from the President, other than, they're working on it.

CDC isn't even giving its typical comfort words. This is scary.

Heard an entire town was shut down.

The leaks board is saying the President is signing a bill to quarantine all sick children.

But the one woman who said it best, called in with the most inner honestly. "No one, unless they have a child, knows what this is like," she said. "There's nothing worse than fearing your own child. I don't know a parent out there who doesn't right now. Something drastic needs to be done. You put your child to bed and haven't a clue if they'll be ripping out your throat in the morning. It's a time bomb. An emotional and heartbreaking time bomb and we are all sitting on it."

Amen to that, Nola thought in response to the woman's words as she drove back to the Laundromat. "Amen to that."

Ripley, WV

'It is weird' was the text that Brady sent to Perseus.
'How so?' he replied.

NODDING – JACQUELINE DRUGA

Brady looked around the grocery store. No one looked at her; in fact, no one looked at each other. There was no music playing, no announcements, the shelves were half empty. She simply told him she'd fill him in when she got home and would be there soon.

She put her phone in her purse.

The water display clearly stated 'one per customer'. There were a lot of handwritten signs around, things were changing fast.

People moved like drones through the store as if they were doing something wrong. She passed two women talking to each other and heard enough of their conversation to know they were talking about a family in town whose child was supposedly infected.

Brady wanted to go to the bigger store, but there seemed to be trouble in the lot, so she turned back for town and hit the small market on the main street.

She left Sammy at home with Perseus. Everything changed so fast. Cyrus was right. It went from normal, to a few reports, to the infection taking over every second of the news. Brady was tired of hearing about outbreaks. People suddenly stopped being friendly and kept to themselves. The local diner … closed.

All of it in a little over a week. Brady had read many of books that depicted a plague or virus wiping out humanity and she scoffed at how fast the illness moved. Now she didn't scoff. She was living it.

Her picture-perfect, small-town community was becoming a poster child for a dystopian world.

What she wanted, and needed, to hear was new info from Cyrus, but he had nothing new to give her. Just that he was working on it and he gave that same update every single day.

Shopping buggy only partially full, Brady decided to check out. In the middle of being rung up, her phone rang, she saw it was Bobby, silenced it, then smiled at the clerk. Brady hated being on the phone in line.

NODDING – JACQUELINE DRUGA

The first words the clerk spoke were when Brady handed her the cash.

"Oh, good, I hate having to explain," the clerk said.

"I'm sorry?" Brady asked.

"You paid in cash." She then pointed to yet, another handwritten sign saying 'cash only'.

"Oh, that." Brady nodded. "I have a brother-in-law who told me the other day that people are going to be cash-only soon. So I was prepared."

"Hopefully not for long."

"Hopefully." Brady smiled, grabbed her receipt and stepped out of line. Before she rolled the cart to her street-parked car, she paused to call Bobby. He answered immediately.

"You okay?" Bobby asked, instead of simply saying hello.

"Yeah, why? What happened?"

"Nothing. Just hate that you didn't answer," Bobby said. "Listen ... where are you?"

"At the store."

"I just got four vehicles in here to work on and gotta get them done ASAP for the county."

"Okay." Brady was curious. Because Bobby worked for the county, to her it wasn't big news.

"They're old and need checked."

"Again, okay."

"They're paddy wagons, Brady. Police wagons. Inside are boxes of restraints."

"Jesus," Brady whispered, her hand nearly dropping the phone.

"They want them cranked out by tomorrow. I called Cyrus, to see if there's something happening. He said things are going to be changing. He couldn't say over the phone, but he said it was time for us to head to your Aunt Jean's."

"No, it's too soon."

"He's gonna be on the news conference tonight. Maybe ... pack the baby."

103

"Bobby, it's too soon," Brady argued. "Cyrus said, forty percent infected, then it was time. It isn't forty percent. Forty percent of the children in this town aren't infected."

"Brady, maybe the wagons aren't just for the infected children."

"I still think it's too soon. Can we talk when you get home?"

"Yeah, I gotta go," Bobby said. "I love you."

"I love you too," she peeped out, before ending the call. It was a strange call and not one she expected.

Brady began to plan as she made her way to the car. Ralph's sister had a secluded farm just near the Ohio–Pennsylvania border. He began sending items there to stock it and the plan was, once Cyrus said infection was at forty percent, it was time to move Sammy. It would be desperate, and desperate times would bring desperate measures.

Brady was seeing scared people, not infected children.

She had a hard time accepting that things were moving that fast. After unloading her groceries, she returned the cart. But ten feet from her car, she heard a 'thump'. Slowly she turned her head.

What the hell? she thought, watching the Toyota parked four down from her, move back and forth. Along with the shaking, there was a smacking and thumping sound.

The car was parked like the others on the street. Front forward to the sidewalk and not parallel. She stared for a moment, then took a step from the sidewalk to the car to see what was going on. Then she noticed it. *Was that blood on the back window?*

Closer, closer …

Thump.

A pair of small hands smacked against the rear passenger window and a split second later, a little boy's face appeared. He couldn't have been older than seven or eight. Brady jolted. His eyes were wide, face pale, and his mouth moved as if screaming. He pounded against the glass.

He moved from that window and rampaged around the interior of the car like a mad dog trapped in the summer heat, trying to get out, trying to get air. Blasting against each window, he tried to find an escape. Splatters of blood appeared with each strike the boy made.

Brady reached for her phone.

"No." A woman grabbed her hand, stopping her. "Please don't call."

Eyes wide, lips moving, Brady looked at the woman. "He's hurt."

"He's sick. He broke free. Oh, God." Her hand shot to her mouth, as she held tight to a bag of groceries. "What am I gonna do? If I call for help, they'll take him," she asked tearfully.

Brady didn't know how to answer.

The woman set the bag on the hood of the car and walked to the rear window.

"Johnny," the woman called. "Honey, please it's mommy."

The boy stopped and just stared at her.

Brady thought for a moment the boy had calmed.

"Yes." She sniffled. "It's mommy. Calm down. Calm down."

The boy backed up, and Brady was certain the boy had finished with his episode, that was until the back window shattered and the boy sailed out. His small frame ejected from the broken window, careened without control into the next car, and plopped lifelessly with a deadened 'thud' to the street.

The woman screamed hysterically.

No one came to help. No one came near. They backed up and ran.

The child was not a foot from Brady, and a pool of blood quickly encircled his head.

The horrified ache in Brady's gut caused an immediate reaction from her stomach, and just as she tried to scream, vomit shot from her mouth and Brady began to choke.

Brady coughed and gagged until she could breathe, everything was surreal. She felt helpless; she looked down to see the woman cradling the dead child, crying from the depths of her soul. The woman's lips kissing the child, calling for her son.

Brady's heart broke and, shaking, she grabbed for her phone.

They were in the middle of the main street. Where were the police? Where were the people trying to help? The curiosity seekers.

It was when Brady made that call, that she received proof that Bobby was right. It was time to go. To do something. Because more than the news led on, or even Cyrus, the sickness or infection was worse than anyone had said.

She realized this not by what happened to the boy, but to the mother. In the middle of reporting the incident to 911, Brady watched as the woman dropped the child. Her eyes rolled to the back of her head and before she fell sideways to the concrete, the woman began to convulse violently.

The young mother was dead before Brady completed the call.

New York, NY

It wasn't working. Despite the fact that New York was determined not to fall in fear to the new infection, people stayed inside.

Half the teachers called off at Jill's elementary school, and no one took the substitute jobs. Rumor was, because the school was in a busy part of town.

The teachers weren't the only ones not reporting. The students didn't show either. In fact, maybe only a third of them did.

Jill was teaching all four, fifth grade classes in one room. Just after lunch, which was held in the classroom, she received a message that school would be cancelled until the crisis was over, to just finish the day and gather personal items when leaving.

Jill sighed in relief. Every day, the fear inside of her increased with every new report. She hated bringing her own children to school, but their suburb school had closed and she couldn't get a single person to watch the twins.

They attended class in the next room. The children were silent, reading a story, when she peered up to the clock. They still had forty minutes left. She wanted to send them home, but there were no buses.

That was another worry, the bus drivers were hard put to do their jobs as well. It seemed as if only people with children took the risk.

Jill wanted to inform the class that there would be no school for a while. Ready to explain, telling them to close their books, place them in their book bags and hold on to them, Jill froze at the sound of breaking glass. It was followed by screeching tires and a crash. Typically, it wouldn't cause her to jolt. Accidents on the street, fender benders, were not uncommon.

The crash, and the kids jumping from their seats to see what was happening, was a once a week thing. But this one sent shock waves through her and chills up her spine. She looked at the window, then turned to the class to instruct them to get back to their seats, but the class hadn't moved.

One boy in the third row looked around. Jill didn't know him, she believed his name was Josh, but she wasn't sure. He looked at the other kids—who just stared.

"Mrs. Gibson?" he questioned with a quivering voice.

Jill examined the students. They didn't react. She held out her hand to the boy. "Take my hand, right now."

He slid from his desk chair and as his fingertips touched Jill's, a horrendous cry rang out from the hall. It was joined by screams on the street and more glass breaking.

As if it were a song, a riot was composing and the orchestra blasted it. It surrounded them and came from all directions. Jill gripped the boy's fingers and yanked him to her, placing her arm around him. She lifted her phone from the desk, putting it in her pocket. Eyes on the students, who were in a frozen state, she shuffled carefully to the door, reached for the handle ...

Slam!

Jill jumped. Something hit against the glass of her classroom door. Josh buried his head into her stomach. She looked at the students, their heads nodded as if they were falling asleep. She reached for the door. Slowly, very slowly, she creaked it open. On the floor by the door, the teacher from the next room, Miss James, thrashed back and forth. Violently her body convulsed, head going back and forth, arms flailing, and foam shot from her mouth. Jill briefly thought they could step over her, and make a dash for safety, but just as she opened the door wider, a child, maybe a second grader, ran down the hall. The girl stopped, spun hard to Jill and in a maddened way, raged toward her.

Jill slammed the door.

The slamming was a loud noise.

It awakened the class.

At that instant, all fourteen children in the room jumped up. Chairs squealed and banged against the floor as they stood up, arms extended outward, confused and enraged. They flung desks and threw books. One child banged his head against the desk repeatedly, while another just ran straight until he ran right to— and out the small window.

Jill placed Josh behind her. She wasn't noticed. Not yet. With Josh squeezed firmly in a protective manner between her body and the wall, Jill inched toward the closet in the back of the room.

She could feel him shake and tremble; she could only imagine how scared he was because she knew how scared she was.

In that fourteen-foot-inching walk, she thought of her children, were they okay? Had they, like the others, turned? Not a few feet from the sanctuary of that closet, with a squeak of his tiny high-top tennis shoes, a little boy spun and faced Jill.

Her eyes connected to his dark eyes. Eyes that had lost their soul.

"Run to the closet," she whispered to Josh. "Now." And she shoved him from behind her.

Just as she did, she turned and ran as well.

Josh dove for the closet and just one foot away, hand reaching for the door, Jill was tackled.

She felt the searing teeth of one child tear into her calf, another pounced on her chest, his hand whipped down, ripping flesh from her face.

Three children had her. One on her leg, another on her chest, and the other had her hand pulling at Jill's open mouth.

In that instant, her life flashed before her eyes. She fought, but was helpless against their rage.

Then Jill heard the 'whipping', a repeated sound and the child biting her leg released, the second one, pulling at her lips, let go, and she was able to push the third from her chest.

She rolled onto her stomach and lifted her head. Josh stood there holding the long wooden chalkboard pointer. He helped her. He had saved her.

In pain, eyes welling with tears, Jill summoned all of her strength, scurried to her feet, grabbed the pointer and shoved Josh into the closet.

She turned around to protect them and as she did, one student in a fury, ran her way. She only wanted to swing the pointer at him. Hit him. But the long, thin, wooden object with a pointed ace-shaped tip … impaled the boy.

It went directly into his gut. Jill screamed, but the child didn't react. In fact, as if he weren't injured at all, he kept coming, impaling the pointer deeper into his body. The tip emerged from his back, yet the boy ran until the entire length of the pointer had traveled through him.

Jill released it, backed up, and closed the closet door. She sat against it, her leg, face, and mouth bleed.

"Mrs. Gibson."

Jill shook her head, holding up her hand. "Thank you. Thank you," she whimpered. "Stay back." She hurriedly reached into her pocket and grabbed her phone. Her fingers trembled, and the phone started to slip from her bloody hands.

She fumbled some, then gripped the phone. She tried to focus, but her vision was blurred. Just as her finger began to press 'call', a searing pain shot through her head. It was the worst pain she had ever experienced. Jill paused, but then continued, she had to. She had to make that call.

Ripley, WV

Two wagons done, two to go and Bobby just wanted to get home. Brady was a mess. She was scared. And Doug, one of the mechanics in his shop, had told him that more than ten kids in town had already been infected.

"Just pack, Brady. Just pack," he told her. "I'll be home soon."

The only reason Bobby stayed to finish the wagon was another client was due in to pick up his car. A side job. Bobby told him if he paid cash, he'd take half off.

The man agreed, and that was all Bobby was waiting on.

He didn't care about the state, the county, his job. He just cared about his family.

Opus called, said he was given orders to close his store. He asked Bobby what he was going to do, when Bobby told him, Opus agreed. He'd help Ralph with preparations to help stock the farm, and he too, would leave immediately.

Just as he was putting in the final spark plug in the old wagon, his phone rang. Typically Bobby didn't answer, but on this day, he did.

It was Cyrus.

"Hello," Bobby answered.

"I don't have time. Turn on the news. Things are bad. You need to pack. You need to go. Things are gonna happen."

Bobby heaved out a breath, dropped his hand cloth and turned to lean against the wagon. "What things."

"Quarantines. Sweeps. Not sure. Heading into a meeting now. Nothing can realistically be in total effect for another two days. After then, traveling will be impossible. Go tonight, go now if you can. And, Bobby, bring Sammy's birth certificate."

Bobby felt as if Cyrus was going to hang up, so he asked, "Is there a cure? Any hope yet?"

"Always hope. No cure. I'm working. I am working so hard."

Click.

Bobby took a second to process what Cyrus said, then he'd call Brady, after her, he would call Ralph.

If things were moving this fast and were bad in his small town, he could only imagine how it was in the bigger cities.

New York, NY

All hell had broken lose in a matter of ten minutes. The newsroom buzzed and clamored, and Tom was in the thick of it.

"You're kidding me, right?" Tom asked, looking over the shoulder of one of his producers to the screen shot. A riot ensued on the streets of Los Angeles, a small community of the big city. Fires broke out, children ran about.

"This is a no-shit situation. Look at the people on the ground." Price pointed.

Tom watched the helicopter shot. It was insane. People lay on the ground, their bodies convulsing, shaking, flopping like fish out of water, as children ran around them. Some even pounced on the downed adults.

Thankfully, there wasn't a clear, close-up shot.

"Run it?" Price asked.

"We have to run it all. But with what?" Tom asked. "What do we have?"

"Too many cities to count. This came to a head today."

Another voice called out from across the room, "Tom?"

Tom turned.

The man held a phone. "National Guard was just mobilized."

"Confirmed?"

"Not by DOD, but by a friend who is in the National Guard. He's going to Allentown, PA."

"Allentown?" Tom cocked back. "Get on this, see where else they are sending them. I need confirmation from the DOD."

"Got it," the man replied.

The response in the form of a religious blaspheme, caught Tom's attention.

"Jesus," Melina gasped out, not two feet from Tom. "Any official word yet?" she spoke into the phone.

112

Tom snapped his fingers and after getting her attention, questioned, "What's up?"

Melina covered the phone and looked at Tom. "FEMA is prepping their disaster camps. A source reports there is movement and trucks at Lexington."

"Stay on that," Tom instructed. "Where, how many, what for. I need that."

Tom did need answers. With the National Guard and FEMA involved, he had a good idea where he could get those answers. Cyrus Conner.

He walked across the chaotic production room and sought his phone. Just as he reached for it, it rang.

Seeing Jill's name, he knew he'd answer but ask her if he could call back. He was prepared for that, to say, 'Can I call you back?' but before he could respond, before he could even say hello, Jill's painful and weak, "Tom." Made him buckle.

"Jill?"

She cried and her words cracked, "I have only a few seconds. I love you."

"Jill."

"I love you. I love the twins. Tell them, I love them. Tell them … find them. Tom …"

Her final word was weak and high pitched. And then he heard the phone drop.

"Jill!" he called out strongly.

From across the room, Price yelled, "Tom!"

Tom ignored him. He listened and his heart pounded. Who was the child crying in the background of the phone call? Who was the child screaming Jill's name in horror. "Jill, please," Tom yelled into the phone.

"Tom," Price called stronger.

"I can't talk!" Tom held up his hand. "Jill." He heard nothing. "Jill!" The line was dead. Pulling it from his ear, he stared at the phone.

"Tom."

Tom squinted. "What the fuck?" He spun hard to Price. "I have a situation, my wife …"

"Where does she teach, Tom?" Price asked with the utmost concern. "Where?"

Oh, God, Tom thought when he saw the look on Price's face. "Hunter Elementary."

Price lowered his head, then lifted his eyes. His lips pursed and he merely pointed to the computer screen. "There's a problem."

Tom saw the chaos on the screen. He looked to the phone in his hand, back to the screen and then, heart aching; mind screaming for his wife, Tom just took off running from that newsroom.

Chapter Thirteen

New York, NY

The twelve children had made their way down a flight of stairs, a long hallway, and to the first floor main office. They had to stop there, so close to the front doors, but they couldn't go. Not yet.

Jenny Gibson led them but not because she wanted to –. It was mainly because everyone followed her and Jerrod. While it is not uncommon for a parent to say their daughter is an old woman in a little girl body, it was correct to say that about Jenny. She was wise beyond her eight years. She and her twin brother looked so much alike with light brown hair, big brown eyes and both small for their age, but she was the thinker and he the reactor.

She wanted to find her mom. That's all she wanted to do, but even though her mom was right in the next room, she and her brother could not get to it. She told him that and he did what Jenny said.

Kids in the school were attacking other kids and, almost instantly, those kids were infected. Jenny found out by accident how not to get attacked. She and Jerrod were in the class when infected children raged in. Scared, she started freaking out and throwing things to keep them away and they ignored her.

'Was that it?' she wondered. Was that the key to not getting attacked? Act like them, don't look at anyone, just throw things, and move a lot?

Jenny and Jerrod did and with that, they made their way to the first floor.

Others followed.

The principal of the school was dead by the secretary's desk. There was a circle of liquid around his mouth and his eyes were open. Jenny looked at him before she jumped over his body and raced into his office.

Once her brother and the other kids were inside, she locked the door.

They stayed low on the floor and were quiet. Jenny was smart enough to know she had to call for help, but when she called 911, she was put on hold. She didn't know her father's number. One of the kids knew his home number, but no one answered.

They had to stay put.

Crawling on the floor, Jenny inched her way to the small window and peered out. There were a lot of people outside, including the police.

"Are they out there?" Jerrod asked.

"Who?"

"The sick kids."

Jenny shook her head. "No, just police and other people."

"Then it's safe. We should run out. The door isn't far. We should just all run out real fast," Jerrod said.

"We can't. They're here because of the sick kids in this school. What if we run and they think we're like them." Jenny shook her head "No, we stay here and stay quiet. They'll come in here soon. We just have to wait."

Jenny turned her back and sat against the wall. She reached out and held her brother's hand. She was scared, really scared, but she couldn't let anyone see it, especially her brother. As long as she had him with her, she was fine and they just had to wait.

Ripley, WV

The 'As Seen on TV' hair brush for tangled hair worked magic on Sammy's messy mane. Brady spent the morning combing her hair more so as not to think about what had occurred. When she returned from the store, she spent time on the phone with Ralph, who was driving a truck full of supplies to Aunt Jean's.

"A lot of canned meat," Ralph said, "but it's better than no food at all, right?'

The plan was that they would leave the next morning at first light.

But Brady, despite 'the tangle free' hair, kept brushing.

Perseus had gone out to two different gas stations to fill cans. Bobby had filled some as well and said they'd take his work van to Jean's.

Brady didn't understand why until Bobby said, 'Just in case we have to hide Sammy.'

Sammy. She was three, so young, too young for the infection, yet she was a child and increasingly over the days, that was a detriment.

"Is my hair pretty?" Sammy asked.

"It's beautiful."

"Are we gonna see Pap?"

"Soon." Brady brushed.

"Why were you crying when you got home?"

"I wasn't." Brady shook her head. "I mean, I was, but it was because I was listening to a song that made me cry."

"That's silly, Mommy."

"I know." Brady placed her lips to her daughter's head. It was time to make her lunch. After placing down the brush, Brady stood and the sound of the television caught her attention. "Mommy will be right back."

Before leaving the kitchen, Brady handed Sammy a box of snack crackers and walked out.

Perseus stood before the television.

"What's going on?" Brady asked.

"All kinds of shit. Look at this."

Brady did. It was the news and it showed police cars. "What is it?"

"Some men just walked into a town and started shooting kids."

Brady gasped. "Were they sick?"

"No, none of them were."

Brady focused on listening to the news for a moment.

'Nine children have been gunned down. That is the tally we have,' the newscaster reported. "The three gunmen are believed to be from this small town just outside of Austin. It's a pretty easy guess what their motive was ...'

"I can't watch this," Brady said to Perseus, taking the remote from his hand. "Turn it off." She aimed the remote.

"No." Perseus stopped her. "You have to be informed of what is happening. This is gonna happen. This is why Cyrus wanted us to leave ... to hide."

Brady's hand went to her face. "Only a week ago ..."

"No," Perseus silenced her. "It's been going on longer than that. Look at the Spanish flu. No one noticed the first wave, but the second killed forty million people in six months. Hitler toppled how many nations using the blitzkrieg?"

"You've been talking to Cyrus."

"I've been studying," Perseus said. "I also believe in his outlandish theory."

"What is that?"

"That every child had this in them. Ever see or read Jurassic Park?" Perseus asked. "They talk about the dinosaurs being genetically created without Lysine. As an insurance – a control that should they need to destroy the species, they just stop giving the dinosaurs Lysine. I think this is nature's Lysine contingency on our species. Every child has it. It's a time bomb waiting to be set off. Nature, God, what have you.... just flipped the switch."

◇◇◇◇

Mon City, PA

Nola divvied up a can of spaghetti and three cold hot dogs. It was their early dinner and all they would eat. Everything she had was in the van ready to go. She wanted to head out to the campsite, but the woman told her they were filled and she was certain the one just before Oglebay, West Virginia was not. In fact, the woman said Oglebay was open to displaced families.

Even though West Virginia wasn't all that far, she didn't want to arrive at the park in the evening. Besides, a lot of things were happening and Nola also didn't want to miss the eight p.m. press conference.

She finally gave in and switched the channel to cartoons. At least the kid networks didn't play the news.

"Mommy?" Carlie asked. "Are we going back to school?"

"Not any time soon, sweetie."

Carlie played with her food. "I don't like hot dogs."

"Just a few bites, Sweetie."

Ben said. "Are we gonna get sick, too?"

Nola's heart dropped. She didn't know how to answer that. She wanted to say 'no', but didn't want to lie because she didn't know.

But Eddie answered, "Mom's gonna try everything she can to keep you from it. That's why we're staying here. There are no kids so no sickness."

Ben smiled and accepted that. Nola reached across their make shift dinner table and ran her fingers through Eddie's hair. "You're so brave."

Eddie shook his head. "No, I'm not."

"More than you realize, you are." Nola lifted her head and turned it to the sound of the phone. It was on the charger across the room. She stood and walked to it.

Looking at the number, she saw it was Tom.

119

"Tom?" She answered with questioned.

"I'm scared, Nola." Tom said. Not a hello. Not another word but that he was scared.

"What's going on?"

"Jill took the kids to school with her today. I'm on my way there. They … they had an outbreak."

Nola gasped. "Are the kids…?"

"I don't know."

"Jill?"

"I … I don't know. All I know is that it's mayhem. Only one adult managed to make it out."

"Oh, God, Tom."

"I just wanted to let you know. I just needed to tell someone."

"I'll be praying. Keep me posted."

She ended her call with Tom and walked slowly back over to the table.

Eddie asked. "Everything okay?"

Nola shook her head. "No. We need to stop right now and say a prayer for Uncle Tom and his family."

"Why?" Ben asked. "Are Jenny and Jerrod sick?"

"We don't know. He doesn't know. We'll find out. But for now …" She extended her hands. "Let's just stop and ask for some help for them."

The small family, around that laundry table with a meager meal, joined hands in prayer.

New York, NY

There was talk about using gas on the students. That was the conversation when Tom arrived. He was one of many parents standing outside of that school, waiting to hear, worried sick. There were police all around. The health department was there positioned by two buses.

No one would tell him anything.

He only knew what he overheard.

The only adult told of how all the children had turned. All? Tom found that hard to believe. Statistically and medically, it was impossible, but, she said as fast as they infected and killed adults, they were infecting each other.

There was no noise and no children coming out. Nothing.

An officer said, "We could storm in but the CDC said that's no guarantee the gas wouldn't kill them if it knocked them out at all."

Then Tom saw that The Zoo personnel had arrived. He turned to a fellow parent and said, "Are you fucking kidding me? The Zoo?"

Eight men unloaded from back of a zoo van. Tom watched as they loaded weapons –, tranquilizer guns. They were going to 'dart' the infected children like rabid animals. That worried Tom. When they knocked them out, then what? What would they do with the kids? There was no cure, no treatment and if Tom's guess was correct, pretty soon there would be no room for them at any hospital.

"Dad," Jerrod said brightly, looking out the window. "I see Dad."

Jenny jumped up as did a few other children, all crowding around the small three by two window.

"I see my mom!" another child yelled.

"Mine, too."

They cheerfully screamed and that caused a ruckus of noise from the hall.

Jenny looked to the barricaded door then back to the window. "Ok, we'll let them know we're here. Maybe they can help us."

Jerrod replied, "Why don't we just run out? Just go. Call out."

"No." Jenny shook her head. "We can't. We have to stay here. We're safe."

"I want my mom," another boy whimpered, a young boy.

Jerrod grabbed the little boy's hand.

Jenny exhaled. "We have to stay put, but, we can call out there." She reached up and pushed the window open. She pressed her face as close to it as she could and hollered. "Daddy! Daddy, we're here. We're fine!"

After yelling, she heard the door slam. Quickly, she turned. Where were Jerrod and the little boy?

"Daddy! We're here. We're fine!" Tom heard his daughter's voice and spun around. Where was it coming from? What window? What room.

She was saying they were fine and Tom had to let authorities know that it was his child calling out. He stepped from the group of parents to the police line.

"Stay back," an officer told him.

"That child yelling … that girl," Tom said. "She's mine."

"We have officers figuring out …"

A voice yelled from the distance. "They're coming out. Back up!"

The door to the school barreled open. Tom looked. A little boy he didn't recognize ran out first followed by … Jerrod.

Behind Jerrod a small pack of children ran full force.

Was Jerrod being chased or was he leading a pack of infected?

He lost all his breath and tried to get by the police officer. He waved out his hand, calling, "Jerrod! Over here."

Jerrod looked.

It was a smile of relief. Tom was sure of it. He saw his father. "Jerrod," Tom called out.

Jerrod changed direction and moved down the street.

His little arm lifted and just as he cried out, "Dad!"

Bang.

No.

Tom was punched in the gut by emotions as he watched a bullet sail into his small son. It smacked center of Jerrod's chest sailing the boy back ten feet.

Another shot. Another child.

The police just fired, they fired upon the kids. They fired until every running child … fell.

"Oh my God, no! No!" With emotional anger and grief, Tom broke through the lines and ran toward Jerrod.

His heart pounded and throat burned. *Oh, God. Oh, God.*

Other parents screamed and ran toward the children. His wasn't the only cry out in pain and agony. Tom's wasn't the only child shot.

Jerrod lay in a pool of blood, his body twisted like a discarded rag doll. In his short run, he prayed hard, but he knew his child was not alive. He knew by looking. He knew by instinct.

With a whimpering groan of pain, Tom dropped to his knees and scooped Jerrod into his arms, bringing the boy's lifeless body to his chest.

His son. His only son. His arms dangled and Tom folded them in to hold every bit of Jerrod. His blood was still warm and flowing. Tom felt it against this own chest as it saturated his shirt.

It was a wave of emotion that caused an uncontrollable sobbing. His lips smeared and pressed hard to Jerrod.

No life at all.

He couldn't squeeze him any tighter, if he could give Jerrod his life, he would.

It didn't make any sense and it hurt more than Tom could handle. Nothing, at that moment was happening around him but his moment with his son, an innocent child. What was he thinking? Was he scared? Did he feel any pain? Tom stayed there for the longest time, holding his child in devastating heartbreak.

But that wasn't the last of it.

Finally everything else came back into focus. People were moving and yelling things. Someone shouted, "Every adult in the building is dead."

"You sure?" Another asked.

"We just checked."

He had been on the street, swimming in his loss for so long, he never knew they had gone into the school. They did a body count. It was over. With Jerrod still in his arms, Tom stood and began to carry him.

Someone in uniform approached him. Tom swatted him away.

"We need to ..."

"Back off!" Tom blasted. "This is my son."

"We need to take him ..."

"You need to take him nowhere." Tom looked at the man. "I need to have him for a little while more."

There was so much going on that Tom banked on the fact that no one else would stop him. Tom didn't know what he was thinking, but he didn't want Jerrod lumped into a pile and taken to a morgue set up. He didn't want him opened or counted like a number. He didn't know what he would do with his son, but for the time being, he just wanted to take him home.

His car was parked near-by, and when he was just about there, it dawned on Tom.

Jenny.

Jill.

He'd have to find them as well.

He opened up the back of his car and, after a kiss to his son, he placed him gently on the back seat, then covered him with his suit jacket.

After closing the door, unnoticed, he walked back toward the school.

They were carrying out bodies, large ones. Tom knew they were the adults. He stopped at every body he passed and on the fifth one, he found her.

She was the only woman he ever loved and he didn't even need to see her body. He knew. She was covered by a plastic tarp and her dangling hand gave away her identity. He'd recognize those wedding bands anywhere.

He still wanted to see her. Tom asked the men carrying her if he could. They cautioned him not to touch her because she was infected. He carefully lifted the tarp. Only a speck of her face was exposed before Tom was filled with a renewed hope.

He dropped the tarp when he heard the distinctive call of his name.

"Daddy!"

Jenny. It was Jenny's voice.

"Daddy!"

Tom moved from Jill's body, not even taking time to process her death. He had to find his daughter. She was calling him.

Then he saw her. She struggled and fought, extending her arms out to Tom, reaching and calling from the arms of a man in a biohazard suit.

He was walking toward the health department bus.

Tom ran as fast as he could to the bus and leapt forward, grabbing the man's arm before he stepped on the bus. His heart raced out of control, his face flushed.

"That's my daughter," Tom told him.

"Daddy! Help." Jenny reached for Tom. Her tiny fingers gripped for his arms, grabbing his skin as the man in the suit yanked her away.

"We're taking her to quarantine."

"Where?" Tom asked.

"Undisclosed."

No way. No how. Tom said nothing, no hero words, no macho rebuttal, he simply took all his sadness and rage along with fatherly protective instincts and formed a fist, driving it into the side of the man, winding him enough to release Jenny.

He grabbed her and she immediately latched her arms and legs tightly to her father. Her arms clung so tightly to his throat she nearly strangled him, but she held on so tightly enough on her own that Tom could make a run for it.

He heard them yell, "Stop him."

Another called out, "Stop or we'll shoot."

But no one did. No one stopped him or shot at him. He felt someone try to grab him, but Tom was so focused on getting to his car, he didn't care.

He opened his SUV door, slid in with Jenny still attached to him, reached sloppily into his pocket for his keys, and started his car.

Jenny cried hysterically on his lap.

Tom shifted gears and then clutched Jenny's head, holding him to her. "Don't look in the back, baby, don't look in the back."

She nodded her understanding within his hold.

Tom moved rapidly. He had to. He checked his mirrors and saw two policemen running his way. He jerked the wheel, peeled out of the spot, and sped down the street.

He didn't care. He didn't stop. He didn't even remove his daughter from his lap. He drove with her right there against his chest.

He drove erratically and fast, making his way from the scene. Once he was several blocks away from the school, he slowed down and took a breath. He checked his rearview mirror. No police followed him.

At least for the moment.

There were a lot of things Tom was unsure of at that time. Would he be caught? Would they follow him? He didn't know what he would do next or even where he and Jenny would go.

That, to Tom, wasn't important.

He had his daughter.

That was all that mattered.

Chapter Fourteen

Washington, DC

There were two parts of Cyrus pushing within him an inner struggle argument - the reasonable scientist and the man who loved his family.

No, this isn't happening.

But it needs to be.

Inner arguments. Turmoil.

When the President said in an emotional, gut response to secure the children who were infected, Cyrus commented sarcastically that the solution wasn't the infected children. It was all of the children.

In one day, they moved on it.

What did Cyrus begin?

In order to save humanity, the infection had to be stopped or contained.

The only way to contain the infection was to contain those most susceptible.

It wasn't possible. No way. No how.

However, when Cyrus returned in twelve hours to the White House, every person that could work on a plan was there, architects, theologians, scientists, and engineers.

The fact was, for every child that was infected, three or more adults were dying. Just kissing an infected child goodnight could cause death.

Without the children, the future was limited. Without adults, the future was done because adults could have more children.

It was an oxymoron proposition – genocide to save the human race.

To Cyrus it was premature. He hadn't even a chance to fully understand what he was dealing with let alone come up with a cure. It was also conceivable, thought slightly, that the infection would just stop.

Problems, aside from the infection, were present. Medical care, means to bury the dead. Not a mortuary was taking infected. The National Guard was not only protecting the communities, they were burning bodies.

Three percent, though not a large margin, were dying from just touching or breathing in the infection.

There were some countries far worse than the U.S., one of which was the UK. They had initiated a medical cleansing;, a free and clear exodus of the cities to anyone over the age of fifteen.

All others stayed behind.

Those who were brought in for infection ... were, as the UK put it, handled in a humane manner.

The Queen of England's twelve year-old grandson was infected. It was announced that he passed peacefully in his sleep.

Cyrus knew better. No child would die of the infection that quickly and in their sleep. They'd die by banging their heads and self-inflicting wounds, but not by sleeping. The infection would take no less than five years to consume the victim.

Cyrus guessed, without fact, that early stages brought one to two outbursts a day. The, outbursts ranging from five minutes to many hours, followed by a hypnotic state with occasional bouts of lucidity – clarity as if the child were not sick at all.

As time passed, days, months, the lucidity would leave. The violent tendencies would increase until finally, at the end of the infection cycle, the child was no less than an enraged creature with no down time.

Enraged until the brain just stopped.

He was back in the room just outside the Oval Office. He passed by huge tables with maps and plans and men talked. It looked like a war meeting. In a sense it was. It was a war against the infection.

The President must have been near the door of his office, because Cyrus heard him blast, "I don't care what the other countries are doing. We aren't in the same spot."

"If we don't show we are taking steps to handle this, it could be considered an act of war." another male voice said from behind the door.

"An act of war" The President repeated.

"Not containing this is threatening humanity. What do I tell them?"

"Tell them, fuck you."

Cyrus balked and in shock repeated the President's words just as the door opened. The President was there with the Secretary of Defense.

"Dr. Donner, you're here. Thank you. We have a press conference," The President said. "I want to meet with you before we go on."

"We?" Cyrus asked. "We?" He followed the President's quick pace.

"Yes, we. We are both speaking tonight."

Cyrus silently grumbled and cringed inside. He didn't think he was there to speak. Yes, he was the head scientist on the case, but not the head of the CDC. That was the Director's job, not his. "Sir," Cyrus called for the President. "While I appreciate the confidence in my ability to convey things to the American People, I think they'll feel more secure of someone in authority speaks about the virus."

"I am," the President said.

"I'm talking medical, virology, pandemic authority stuff. The direct of the CDC ..."

"Is dead." The President stopped walking. "Dead." He nodded. "He kissed his child." On those words the President continued and Cyrus had no choice but to follow.

Cyrus was honest.

Not camera or emotionally ready, he aphorized to the press and the cameras. "I'm still dealing with a personal shock," he said, thinking about the Director of the CDC and how he hadn't even known or was told. He didn't speak about it. He just continued.

He spoke of the origins – of where and when it started in 1967.

What it did back then, how it mutated, and then how the transmission mutated. He was informed to keep it simple, keep it layman and keep it truthful with no sugar coating.

Unlike any other infection, plague, or virus, Tantrum, Nodding as it was originally called never left. It was always around and it always infected.

It progressively gained strength.

Its infection rate grew until nearly entire communities of children were stricken. But that was always 'over there' and now it's here. It's everywhere.

Nature built it and man was fighting it, but time was the enemy.

For it no longer stopped at the children. It jumped, slammed, and killed any adult exposed to it without a chance or a fight.

A reporter raised her hand and identified herself before asking. "You said bacteria. Is this strain antibiotic resistant

"Yes and no. We have to assume it is because it moves so quickly no antibiotic has time to work."

"Is there any cure?" another reporter asked. "Any inkling?"

"I'm trying, but we can't cure it. We have to stop it," Cyrus replied. "I may, one day, be able to beat the bacteria, cure it in a sense, but that's not what we need. We need a block. We need something to stop the bacteria from entering the bloodstream because once it hits a child, it goes right to the brain. It immediately starts doing damage. One to, two, five days later the child turns. The damage is irreversible. If we had the ability to have brain matter regenerated then we would have defeated

Alzheimer's, but we don't have that technology. So even at best, even by stopping it, any child already infected has been damaged. This thing eats away and eats away until …" Cyrus paused. "Until …" He exhaled and looked to the President. "That's … that's all I have."

President Henry Collingsworth nodded and then took the podium. At that point a reporter called out his question to Cyrus.

"So it's deadly?"

The President breathed heavily into the microphone. "I think the fact that it is irreversible is an answer, don't you?" He held out a hand. "Please. Just give me a moment."

Known as America's most approachable President, Henry presented no less at that conference. Young, down to earth, he wore a button down shirt, sleeves rolled up, no tie, and the shirt wasn't even tucked in.

He cleared his throat and leaned forward against the podium, hands semi folded. "I looked at my daughter, Anna, before I came here. She's nine, as most of you know. I looked at her and thought, as privileged as her life is right now, as much security as I can have around her, I can move her to the highest mountain or deepest bunker, but that doesn't protect. I can't … protect her, because a bug, a sneeze, anything can give it to her. Now if this thing reaches its potential as it has done in the small communities overseas then I have a ten percent chance she won't get sick. Dr. Donner …" He motioned his hand to Cyrus. "He told me ten percent are naturally resistant – ten percent. It's nothing to jump up and down about but it is something to hold on to."

The President took a moment and continued. "But here is where my concern lies. Ten percent of our future is guaranteed not to get sick. But if ninety percent is infected and the germs they carry kill the adults, who will protect that ten percent? Who?" He lifted then dropped his hands. "There's a threshold number, a doomsday number. Once we hit that, it's done. It'll keep going until it hits everyone it can and the infected infect everyone they can. There are some countries that have reached this number and some have not. I can't concern myself with that. I have to concern myself with here and now and our country. They aren't coming here. Have you seen any planes?" He shook his head.

There was absolute quiet in the press room.

"I could have done this heart wrenching, motivating speech from the Oval Office, pumping sunshine up your ass and filling you with false hope, but who am I kidding? Look around. This room is usually standing room only. There's what ... twenty of you here? Truth is we have skeleton crews now running utilities. People are afraid to leave their kids and I don't blame them. Wall Street won't open tomorrow so we can say goodbye to the financial infrastructure. That is our least of our concerns."

He continued, "This is a do or die, last stand, last hope and ditch situation and tomorrow we move on it full force. Some will grasp for it, some will not. It's a long planned effort that will happen in stages. Each stage representing a movement toward that threshold I mentioned. It is what needs to be done. This thing is beyond our youth. It kills every adult it touches in minutes ... minutes. The higher the number of infected, the harder we move the plan. This isn't personal. This is survival and mankind's future. Every country is handling it differently. This is how we'll handle it." He saw a reporter raising his hand in the back of the room, the. The President nodded at him to take his question.

"What is the doomsday threshold number?" he asked.

"Fifty-one percent," Henry answered. "Right now we're at twenty-five, maybe more, and it's increasing by the day. Truth is, we don't have the medical resources to handle the twenty-five percent, let alone more than that. There's no treatment. Some anti -seizure medication help, but not always. So here's the plan. We are asking all parents to keep their children in their own home and keep a diligent watchful eye for the symptoms. Travel with children is not permitted. Road blocks and checkpoints are being established now. Should your child be infected, you at no time should touch the child without gloves or a mask. FEMA is opening up its emergency camps and shelters. Again our medical facilities are not taking children. If you feel you do not want to handle or cannot handle your infected child, you are to bring him or her to a medical site set up for this. If one is located out of your city, there are ways to get help."

President Collingsworth told of the red flag, white flag system. In order for the National Guard to gauge the infected homes, parents were urged to place a white cloth of flag on their porch or out there windows. If they needed the child taken for help, they were to place a red flag.

It sounded cold, but it was the only way to control the situation and the children.

He then told of the cities.

Five cities on the East Coast were being evacuated and construction would commence... just in case.

The cities would be isolated, contained, and protective walls placed around them. The areas around them would be flattened. That was a last resort –. That was the last measure.

It was the President's hope that the first few steps would prevent that.

"At what point ..." A questioned was asked. "Will the cities be used?"

"A sixty percent infection rate. We believe that at that point we're losing sixty percent of the adults as well."

"So the infected are going to be placed in walled cities? We are just going to lock the children in there until they kill themselves or die?"

"We're not putting the infected in there," The President said, "We're relocating the healthy, the future."

It was the only time that a loud eruption of voices occurred in that room.

The President held up his hand. "At some point, if it gets to that, there has to be a segregation of age. It has to be ... or this is all moot. It will take over and wipe us out. I've been told this thing has to be dead and gone for five years before we can breathe easily and that no more children will be infected. Then… we will have seen the last of it. It's a complicated situation and I just urge the American people to comply, to do what they can. Thank you."

He started to step away and then someone else called out. "It's rumored that other countries are euthanizing the infected. Is this a step the U.S. plans to take?"

The President stopped and returned to the podium.

"There is no cure, there is no treatment and, for the infected, there is no turning back." He lowered his head. "Euthanasia is thought of as morally wrong and also illegal. At this time, if a parent feels it is the only option that is their decision to make. No repercussions. That option is there, but it is … an option, not a requirement. As a parent, I couldn't make that decision. If I had to, it would be unbearable. Allow your child to live violently and still have her or sleep peacefully – quality versus quantity. I don't know a single parent who would make that decision lightly and, as a leader and a father, I would not impose that on them. That's why we're doing what we are doing."

The President said a few more words, a repeat of things he said before. He took only a couple questions, again repeating things, and then he left to work on the plan, and then be with his family.

Cyrus had a sense of foreboding at that conference but he couldn't think about that. Like the President, he had a job to do and after the conference, he returned to the special lab they had set up for him in Washington, DC.

135

New York, NY

"What have I done?" Tom wept on the phone to Nola.

"You did what you had to do. You did what I would have done, what any parent would have done."

"Oh, God, Nola, he didn't deserve it. He was running to me, calling me. *Calling* me. Looking so glad to see me …" He had to stop. "He didn't deserve this."

"I'm sorry. I'm so sorry."

"Jill's gone. Jerrod's gone. What am I going to do?"

"You have Jenny, you have her. Protect her. Leave the city."

"I can't. I have to be responsible. Jenny was exposed. I have to wait the five days. That'sThat what Cyrus said."

"Then what?"

"I don't know. I don't even know what to do with my son."

And he didn't.

Tom was at a loss. He drove home after the school incident. Jenny finally realized Jerrod was in the back seat and kept asking why Tom wasn't taking him to a hospital.

There was nothing a hospital could do for the child. The fist-sized burn with a bullet hole in his chest was proof of that.

He couldn't take him to a funeral home or the morgue.

He'd figure it out after he stopped. Tom thought about burying him in the yard, but how does one do that? How does one just dig a hole in the back yard and place their flesh and blood in there? Where was the ritual – the funeral? It felt cold to do that to someone he loved more than life itself.

He held Jerrod often, despite how stiff and cold his body became.

A part of Tom hoped that maybe it was all a bad dream. Maybe if he prayed hard enough his son would open his eyes.

Finally, not knowing what to do with Jerrod, Tom wrapped him tightly in a blanket and put him in his room.

His grief was so overwhelming, Tom wasn't thinking clearly. After a rest maybe he could process his thoughts. His face felt drawn as if gravity had pulled down the side of his mouth and there was no control over that.

He cried.

He couldn't stop crying.

Weeping was a better word.

After feeding Jenny a late night supper of soup, Tom took to the back deck with a bottle. Jenny slept on the small outdoor couch with a blanket and Tom just stared out, sipping, staring, and crying, His head pounded. He couldn't even appreciate what he had left because he was downing in his loss.

The next day would bring answers, he hoped. He caught only a moment of the President's speech, but turned it off. He didn't care.

He just didn't care.

Tom wanted quiet like he was used to when he sat on his deck but that wasn't to be found. Crying, screams, sobbing, gunfire, and crashes rang out, echoing in the night. The suburban neighborhood sounded like a war zone.

It was.

Tom felt finished. He was done. If it wasn't for Jenny, he would have taken a bottle of sleeping pills.

But for then, he just stared out, listening to the anguish cries of parents. He wasn't alone in his suffering, not at all.

Jenny stirred and it made Tom jolt.

He shifted his eyes to the couch and Jenny sat up.

Admittedly he was worried. Had she turned? Was she sick? If she was, it was over –, completely over for Tom.

Jenny sat up, looked at him, and then dropped the blanket. She rubbed her eyes and sniffled. 'Daddy?"

"Oh, sweetie, come here." Tom put down his glass and held out his arms.

Jenny whimpered and raced to him, immediately climbing on his lap. "Daddy, I'm so sad."

"I know … me, too." Tom kissed her.

"I miss Mommy. I want Mommy. I want Jerrod."

"Me …" Tom choked on the words. "Me too."

Her legs tucked under her body and pressed against his chest. Tom wrapped his arms tightly around her.

"Am I going to get sick?" she asked.

Tom wanted to say no. He wanted to say he prayed she wouldn't but he couldn't. He placed his lips to her head. "I'm going to do my best to protect you, baby. I promise." He kissed her again. "I promise."

In his sadness and grief, lost and broken, Tom held on to the only thing he had left.

He held on tight.

Chapter Fifteen

September16

Mon City, PA

There was nothing on the television until ten in the morning, nothing to let Nola know what was going on. News was sporadic and she embraced each word spoken.

She couldn't even get an Internet signal.

So much had changed, so quickly, in just the couple weeks since she first heard of the strange illness.

It was time to go. It was, time to head to Claysville although Nola wasn't certain that she'd even be able to get there considering the news reported random roadblocks and checkpoints.

The kids were washed and ready to leave the Laundromat. The van was packed with the little food they had and jugs of water she had filled. To her surprise, the door opened.

Mrs. Rogers, an elderly woman who came to the Laundromat weekly to do her sheets, walked in. "We're closed," Nola said. "I'm sorry."

"No, I'm not here to do laundry." She stayed near the door, her eyes shifting to the children. "I'm here because Bill and I are leaving. We're headed to West Virginia to our camp, away from folks, away from … from children."

"I understand."

"The camp ground assured us it was over fifteen only. They … they're evacuating Pittsburgh. It started at six AM. My nephew was moved out. I think it's gonna be one of those cities the President talked about."

"Why do you say that?"

"Other than the evacuation, my nephew said trucks were moving into town in masses. Construction trucks."

"That is scary."

"Have you been out today, Nola?"

"No, I haven't been."

"Seems someone rolled in here during the night, posted all kinds of flyers about what to do, where to go, and fast setup medical facilities. If you want to get any food, you may wanna head to the Foodland before they run out."

"I'm kind of on a fixed income right now. We have to travel to Claysburg to find a place to stay."

"That's why I'm here," the woman said, "not to be your news alert, but ... I know you and the kids are living here."

"Not for long. We have to be out today. That's why we're going to Claysville."

"Nola, sweetie, it's bad out there and in my eighty years I have never seen it like this. I don't suppose much will be left when this is all said and done. I don't suppose I'll even come home. So ..." She reached out her hand and placed a set of keys on a washer. "Until I do, you and them children can stay in our house."

At that second, Nola was overwrought with emotion. She couldn't even speak.

"We took all the food. I'm sorry."

"No, no that's ... I don't know what to say."

"Say you'll stay away from others with those kids. Keep them away. Keep them safe."

"I will. Thank you. Thank you so much. We had nowhere to go ..." Nola stepped to Mrs. Rogers and she inched back. Nola understood the elderly woman's apprehension. After wringing her hands, Nola nodded and smiled a tear-filled smile. "Thank you."

"Good luck to you." Mrs. Rogers took a second to look at the kids then walked out.

"Holy cow, Mom." Eddie moved forward. "Did Mrs. Rogers just loan us her house?"

"Yes." Nola spun around. "Yes, she did. Can you stay with the kids?"

"Sure."

"I'll be right back," she spoke with renewed enthusiasm. "I'm gonna head to Foodland and get what I can. We don't need that gas money or traveling money. I'll be back. I'll be right back." She moved Ben and Carlie to the back room for safety's sake and headed out the door with a rush.

People all around were dying, but the kind deed of Mrs. Rogers just left Nola knowing that humanity wasn't dead ... not yet.

West Virginia – Ohio Border

Brady was almost convinced that the 'border checkpoints' were a myth. They didn't see one at all in West Virginia. The intermittent news talked about them and the cities on the east coast that were being quarantined. One newscaster called it an exodus and one he would never imagine seeing.

All that painted a different picture than Brady and Bobby witnessed in their drive to Ohio.

When they left Ripley, they didn't see any of the massive amounts of white or red flags that were spoken about on the news. They saw maybe three. Was Ripley really not that affected or were people just not reporting?

No one was on the street. No one was leaving. The noisy work van was the only sound as it rolled through the echoing, dead quiet streets of the small town.

Brady didn't get it. Bobby was a mechanic. Why did the van sound so bad?

141

There was some traffic on the road but they maintained a good speed. Sammy stayed low in the back of the van with Perseus. She had to. They couldn't take a chance. Martial Law had gone into effect and one established rule was no one under the age of fifteen was permitted to leave his or her town. It was the Government's way of keeping things in check, in order, and accountable.

But the free and clear path to Aunt Jean's became a parking lot of traffic thirty miles before the Ohio border. It was so jammed packed they had to shut down the van, only turning it on occasionally to cool down.

Most people wandered outside like it was a family picnic.

Brady knew they were all in the same situation, but one hidden child, one child that could turn, could make the packed roadways a disaster. She hated that Bobby walked a few cars up to give them gas. She hated it for two reasons. One, he was away from the van and the other, people knew he had extra gas. That made them a target in desperate situations.

Stay close … stay safe. Although Brady witnessed that child sailing through a closed window, she wasn't certain about the glass.

"It's like a hundred degrees in this van," Perseus said. "Can I just get air?"

"For a moment, but stay close." Brady instructed and jumped when her phone rang. It was Ralph.

"Hey there," he said. "Any word? How far out are you guys?"

"We're stuck in a parking lot of traffic."

"Border?"

"Yep."

"That's why I was calling. Was gonna instruct you to get off any county or state maintained road. Just heard about the checkpoints."

"Do you know if they are effective?" Brady asked.

"Nothing really is steady on the news. Blips here and there," Ralph said. "But they are arresting people hiding children."

Brady's heart dropped. "Are they searching the vehicles that thoroughly?"

"I don't know. Keep her hidden."

"We'll hide her pretty good if need be. Are you going to Aunt Jean's?"

"I'll be there. I'm loading up a truck, bringing it down to you guys, and then I'm probably gonna head back, close up shop, and bring one more round of stuff."

"Close up shop?" Brady asked surprised.

"Yeah, sweetheart. I had half my employees not show up today. They just didn't show. Even though I handle one of the top foods of the apocalypse, no one's working. I did send a message out to my employees that if they needed food to see me."

"That's very nice of you."

"Yeah, well, wouldn't have the product in storage if they didn't work so damn good. Don't want them holding up without anything."

"Well, keep me posted. We aren't getting anything on this radio."

"Will do. Be careful. I love you."

"I love you, too." Brady hung up the phone and noticed Perseus who was too far away. "Damn him."

"What's wrong, Mommy?" Sammy asked.

"Nothing sweetie. Uncle Perse isn't listening."

"I'm hot."

"I know."

Brady turned her head when Bobby's door opened. "All good."

"Yeah." Bobby looked over his shoulder. "Sammy, sweetie, you have stay further back, ok?"

"Can Mommy sit back here with me now?"

Brady nodded. "Yes. Bobby, tell your brother to get his ass closer to the van. He's way up there."

Bobby peered closer to the windshield. "What the hell is he doing? Is he talking to those people by that car?"

From her viewpoint Brady saw Perseus. He moved back and forth, spinning around. "Something is wrong."

"You're right," Bobby said and opened the door.

Not much frightened Bobby to the point his heart raced and he felt that wave of nervous fear, but he was scared when he jumped from the van.

All he saw was his little brother, the boy who was no less than a son to him, dropping to the ground, his arm extended under a car.

Was he being grabbed? Bitten?

Screaming out, "Perseus!' Bobby flew to his brother, weaving in and out of cars.

Why wasn't anyone trying to help him?

As soon as he arrived to his brother, ready to reach down and grab him, Perseus emerged from under the car.

The young man had a huge grin on his face.

Out of breath, Bobby said, "You okay?"

"Yeah, check this out." Perseus held up a puppy; a really tiny and young puppy. "I saw him, and chased him and …"

"You had me worried. I thought, something happened, that maybe …"

Perseus laughed and that annoyed Bobby.

"It's not funny. I want you near the van. You hear me. Don't wander again."

"I saw it and had to get it."

With a grumble, Bobby laid his hand on Perseus' back, turned him from the people that had gathered, and walked with him back to the van.

The left side of the double back doors opened to the van and Bobby stood there with Perseus. "Don't make me tie you up," he said to his brother as he climbed inside behind him and shut the doors.

Brady was in the back with Sammy. "You scared me," she told him.

"I know. I'm sorry. I saw this and had to get him for Sammy." He extended the dog.

Sammy smiled widely. "A puppy." The second Perseus placed the animal in Sammy's arms, the dog went crazy in a happy way and Sammy giggled.

Bobby reached down and swiped his hand over the dog's face. "He's probably hungry. That's why he's licking her. We have canned ham. The dog is gonna have to like that."

"Sweetie," Brady said. "You have to come up with a name."

"George." Sammy replied without hesitation. "I want to call him George."

"Why?" Brady asked.

"George was the man that lived down the street, remember? He hurt his legs when he was at the war," Sammy answered innocently. "You said he was brave. He got hurt protecting us."

Brady replied, "Boy, you remember good."

"I like George. He didn't leave his porch and you'd sit with him. This is George." She petted the dog. "He's brave. He will protect us when he gets big, Mommy."

Perseus spoke up, "I thought that immediately when I saw him. He's little like Sammy. Keep them together. He's a German Sheppard. He'll watch her good." Perseus crouched before Sammy and looked over his shoulder at Brady then to Bobby. "I'm sorry I scared you guys, but I thought this little guy was worth it. I thought saving him was symbolic, you know. He was hiding and now he is safe."

Perhaps Perseus was right, that George the dog could serve as protection. Brady looked down to her daughter, holding that puppy as if she received the greatest gift in the world. And with the way the world was, every bit of protection was good.

New York, NY

Tom hoped and prayed with everything he had that all the events of the day before were nothing but a dream. But the reality of it hit him when he woke on his deck, his daughter Jenny curled up next to him. A thin of haze of smoke hovered in the sky and a quiet took over the city.

The night before the air was filled with screams, cries, and gunfire.

His stomach twitched with the thought of all that happened.

His wife and Jerrod were gone. His precious daughter could be next and there was nothing Tom could do about it. Things had changed. Jill was killed. Her body taken by the authorities yet Tom never received a call about her, not that he could have done anything. He couldn't.

As much as he loved his wife, he had to worry about his child that remained. What would he do with her? Where would he go? How could he protect her? Could he even keep her safe?

He slid from the chase lounge chair and Jenny, in a deep sleep, rolled over into his spot. Tom covered her then kissed her. He had to figure out what to do with Jerrod.

His entire being ached with an emotional sadness that turned into a physical pain. After opening the sliding glass doors to the deck, he turned on the television. Work hadn't even called him and he realized why when his news station wasn't even on the air.

A black screen with typed words scrolled by in an eerie silence telling people where to take the ill and where to take the deceased.

Red flag if you need help.

White flag if you're fine.

If you had a body in the house, you were to take it to one of the listed locations or to the curb, wrapped in plastic, a shower curtain, or drapery.

Really? Tom thought as he read the words. Put the body of a child or family member out to the curb like the trash?

If Tom could, he would bury Jerrod right on the property, but the problem was Tom lived, like millions of others, in a concrete jungle. His house wasn't really a house, but a row house and his backyard, once a patch of grass, was filled with concrete and a pool.

What to do with his son.

Jerrod's death was a hard reality that hit Tom again when he stepped closer to the boy's bedroom. Despite placing the air conditioning on high and windows open some, the smell permeated the second floor.

It crushed Tom. A child, a mere child, running in hope, shot down by mistake. His body wasn't even getting the respect it deserved and there wasn't anything Tom could do about it.

Before seven a.m., Tom had called fourteen funeral homes, all of which denied the body and all of which referred Tom to one of the many mass burial places.

They weren't burials. They were graves; a big difference.

He envisioned Jerrod running, smiling, riding his bike, and opening gifts at Christmas. Then he was slapped with the vision of his dead son.

No matter how badly things smelled, Tom held him again, crying once more before Jenny woke. He had to figure out what he was going to do.

Jerrod was only eight and thin, maybe fifty pounds. Tom found a box in the basement, one that was big enough to hold

147

Jerrod's body. It didn't have a top, but that didn't matter. Tom put the box in the back of his SUV and before he put Jerrod in there, he found and layered everything cold and icy he could.

Meat, ice, vegetables, he put in the bottom of the box.

Using anything he could find to keep it cold. He carried Jerrod to the car and it broke his heart, but he put the boy in the box, and then covered him.

It was a desecration of his memory. Jerrod deserved more and there was nothing Tom could do. He wasn't putting out a flag or putting his child on the curb for the next pick up.

As much as Tom didn't want to let the child go, as much as he wanted to keep holding Jerrod, he couldn't. Things were bad and he had to move on. He had to focus on Jenny.

After packing food for his daughter and other items, Tom carried her, still sleeping, to the car.

Where they would go, he didn't know, but instinctively he knew how it would all end up.

The full tank of gas dwindled as Tom drove for hours. Jenny stirred in the front seat and woke up, exuding an abundance of sadness. She looked to the back of the SUV, whimpered once, and curled up against the door.

She admitted hunger not long after she woke but barely nibbled on dry cereal.

Tom's choices were limited. He was pretty much stuck on Manhattan Island and traffic out of New York was backed up. People started abandoning cars and walking.

No child was getting out of New York, at least not for a while.

No matter how many places Tom stopped, and he personally stopped at the same funeral homes he called, they told him the same thing. Go to Central Park.

Central Park.

He knew that the Mayor was trying. He really was. He had lost his two grandchildren to outbreaks, both having suffered life threatening injuries during their tantrums.

Too many dead not and enough hands to bury. Decisions had to be made.

But Central Park?

Its beauty was undermined by the hovering death that was everywhere.

Against what he wanted to do, it was Tom's only option with Jerrod. How does one just pull into a park and hand over a child's remains to be placed in a hole with countless other children and adults.

He didn't have the sickness but it didn't matter. The poor child was treated the same. There was no way to even cipher through the emotions Tom was feeling over it all. True heartbreaking turmoil.

The sound of heavy equipment carried to Tom as he neared to the park. Unable to move any closer, he was instructed to pull over and park.

"I have my son and he ..." Tom tried to tell the soldier.

"Check in table is there. I am sorry for your loss."

Sorry for my loss? Tom thought. The soldier didn't have a clue.

Or maybe he did. Tom didn't know his circumstance. But Tom did know, finally, how big this thing actually was when he saw the parents huddled together in sadness, walking from tables. That would be Tom, looking lost and, looking guilty as they did. They felt guilty for having left their child there. Tom knew he'd feel the same way. He already did.

"Daddy? Are we just leaving Jerrod here?" Jenny asked with whimpering words.

"Yeah, baby, we are."

"But what about a funeral? He needs a funeral."

"Yeah, he does. But ..." Tom swallowed the lump in his throat. "But this is the way it has to be now."

"Then will we find Mommy? Are we going to bring Mommy here?"

"I don't know where Mommy is. It's just you and me now, baby."

Her blonde hair fell forward when she nodded her head then lowered it.

"Stay here," Tom instructed.

"I don't want to. I'm scared. What if someone thinks I'm sick and ...?"

"No." Tom shook his head. "That won't happen." But Tom wasn't sure. He wasn't sure about anything. He squeezed her hand. "You're right. Come with me. Can you be a big girl about it?"

"Yes."

It was time to bring his son's remains to be buried. Holding Jenny's hand, he walked to the back of his SUV and opened the hatch. Before he lifted Jerrod's body, he stopped and prayed. It was the only thing his poor son would have over a burial.

In his mind, Tom envisioned a preacher or priest sprinkling holy water over the mass graves. Something. Anything. He hoped.

There was a reason for it all. Tom just prayed for understanding and protection for his daughter, strength too, he needed strength.

With a crying daughter at his side, he lifted Jerrod from the box. His body was rigid and cold and, despite how hard Tom tried to cradle him, his limbs resisted.

With Jerrod against his chest and holding Jenny's hand, Tom walked the block to the check-in tables set up on the edge of the park.

A beautiful setting for such an ugly occurrence.

"I'm sorry for your loss," was the greeting Tom received by the man in the gas mask.

Really? Really? Were they programmed to say it or did they mean it?

Tom nodded, "Thank you."

The man in the gas mask asked for Jerrod's name, date of birth, and social security number. As if it would matter. All the children seemed to be infected so quickly, were they able to log it all?

Beyond the man, someone was hammering two pieces of white wood together to make a cross. Tons of crosses. It made Tom sick to see them.

"We'll take him now," The man in the gas mask said.

"Are they …are they for the children?" Tom asked of the crosses.

"For everyone buried here," The man replied. "After each grave is full, we'll do our best to place a marker with a name on it."

"Where should I lay him?" Tom asked.

The man pointed to a truck.

An ache seeped through Tom's being. He could see the mounds of bodies in the truck, all small. How could he do it? How could he just place his flesh and blood, a child he adored into the back of a large military truck? He had to. Each step hurt. He held tight to Jenny's hand and Jerrod's body.

At the truck, he paused, squeezed Jerrod tightly against him. "I love you," he whispered. "I love you so much." He pressed his lips hard to Jerrod's head. "Daddy loves you. I'm sorry. I'm sorry." He sniffed and slowly laid him down. "I am so sorry." Once more, Tom leaned forward and kissed his son, leaving his lips there until the moisture from his eyes seeped to his chin. Releasing a heart wrenching single sob, Tom closed his eyes tightly, lifted Jenny into his arms, and walked away.

"Sir?" the man called as Tom cleared from the truck.

Tom stopped.

"Your paperwork and receipt."

He looked over his shoulder and then, after a breath, Tom stepped back, grabbed the paper the man extended, and walked away.

A receipt. A receipt for his son? Jerrod was more than just an object or laundry left for the dry cleaners. He was more than something that required a receipt. Unfortunately, with so many children dying and turning, Jerrod, like the others, was just a number.

That broke Tom's heart all over again.

Tom became instantly just like the parents he saw as he approached the table. Sad and guilt ridden.

Crumbling the paper in his hand and holding Jenny to his chest, Tom moved toward his SUV and didn't look back.

Chapter Sixteen

Mon City, PA

The three tones followed by the message, "We're sorry. All circuits are busy. Please try your call again later.' saddened Nola and worried her as well. Her brother, Tom, was the only family, outside of her children, that she had and the last she spoke to him, his son had died as well as his wife.

Now Nola couldn't even get through to him and see how he was doing. It wasn't all the phones. It was Tom's area. It had to be. Nola was able to call the Laundromat without a problem. Then again, when she called Eddie from the Foodland, it started a chain of events in Nola's mind.

Eddie said, "Good thing we have a landline, huh, Mom. Wonder if the Rogers have a landline because when the power goes, so will the phones."

When the power goes?

Nola took that for granted. The outbreak only started three weeks earlier, but loss of power made perfect sense.

Workers were calling off in droves. How much longer would it be before the utilities went and then all essential services?

Fall was just around the bend. How would they stay warm? Get gas?

No power, no heat.

Then it dawned on her. No power meant no way to charge Eddie's wheelchair.

The lights flickered at the Foodland and it sent an immediate panic through Nola. She worried about the kids, her brother, and she was devastated by the news of her nephew. To her, the world was falling apart. But Nola was used to not having much, so she had an advantage.

After getting fifty dollars' worth of groceries, food that a month earlier would have cost thirty, Nola stopped by the railroad tracks. She knew that they had been building a new storage facility there and she needed a piece of wood, something to make a ramp so Eddie could get up the two steps into the Rogers home.

She struck out there and finally found something that would work from the renovation site of the Transfiguration Church.

The board was heavy and Nola almost was unable to carry it.

Her next outing would be to find a wheelchair as a backup, but that would have to wait. She had already been gone hours. Time away from Eddie, Ben and Carlie wasn't an option. Eddie was days from his sixteenth birthday and she was confident that he would not get the illness, but Ben and Carlie were prime age. The news reported the easiest infected were between the ages of five and ten.

Seventy, maybe eighty percent.

Nola never had much luck.

Eddie was her oldest and held a special place in her heart. It pained her to think of how hard life was for him and how much more difficult it would be. Nola hated that she had to lock Ben and Carlie in different rooms from Eddie, but it was a chance she couldn't take.

Her instructions to Eddie were to talk to them through the door. Keep talking.

Unresponsiveness was the first symptom, then nodding, then … Tantrum.

Each day, every second was frightening for Nola. Would it be the one? Would her children even wake up the same? She prayed they'd be spared, but she wasn't confident.

Despite the fact that Foodland was busy, the streets weren't. Nola was able to pack up the children in the van, along with her belongings, without drawing attention. Not that she was doing anything wrong, but people had hostility and fear toward children.

She only wanted to protect hers.

The Rogers' home was four blocks from the Laundromat and on Main Street, not far from the Tasty Twist. In fact, Nola saw the military trucks in Tasty Twist, almost as if they were setting up a headquarters there. That struck her as strange considering the hospital was only a mile away. Plus Mon City wasn't a booming metropolis. It was an old town with many seniors.

The home was older and large. Since there was no high or low side of the street, the driveway was located behind the house.

It was a blessing that Nola was grateful for and hoped it afforded her and the kids the chance to escape the epidemic and the craziness the world was thrown into.

Ben and Carlie were excited about living in the Rogers' home. Days in the Laundromat had taken their toll on them and they had become accustomed to being separated and watched. How sad it was to Nola to hear them talk excitedly about being locked in a room instead of a closet.

When would it be over? For Nola, one day it could be. But for Tom it would never be over. Before unloading the kids, Nola tried unsuccessfully to reach her brother again.

"Nothing?" Eddie asked.

"I can't even get it to ring." Nola looked at her low battery power then set down her phone.

"Did you try texting?" Eddie asked.

"If I can't call, I can't text."

"Yeah, but the moment he gets a signal, even if it's only a second, he'll get your text."

Nola hadn't thought of that. She smiled at her son and thanked him. She would do that. She would send Tom a text. First she'd get the kids inside then she'd call again. Nola felt helpless. She sensed her brother needed her and there was nothing she could do but keep trying to reach him.

Ohio Border

Four hours and most of the 'in tank' gas later, Bobby and Brady made it to the front of the check in line. The highway was blocked on both sides by military trucks, soldiers from the National Guard, and yellow roadblock horses.

"My stomach is doing flip flops," Brady said as they pulled up for their turn at the search.

"We're fine." Bobby rolled down the window.

"Identification please," the soldier asked as he looked with shifting eyes into the van.

Bobby reached into his back pocket, "Long day for you?" He handed the license.

"I've seen better." The soldier smiled. "West Virginia. Where are you going in Ohio?"

"Medina County," Bobby replied. "Her father lives there."

"Just you two?"

"No. My brother is in the back. He's eighteen. He has ID if you need it. Perse ..." Bobby aimed his voice. "Pull out your license."

"No children under fifteen?"

Bobby shook his head.

The soldier gave a nod. "Sir, we do have to check the van."

"Absolutely. I understand."

"Turn off the engine and step from the vehicle please. I need to see both of your hands – only one of you."

Bobby turned off the ignition, lifted his hands, and the soldier opened the door for him. As he stepped out, he saw

156

NODDING – JACQUELINE DRUGA

another soldier approach. He was scared. Did someone report them since? He didn't see anyone else holding up their hands. Then again, Bobby didn't pay too much attention until they were close and there weren't any vans like Bobby's.

With one soldier watching Brady, Bobby walked around the back of the van with the other. After receiving a nod, Bobby opened up both sides of the van.

At first the soldier stood protectively to the side then moved into closer to the view the van.

Perseus sat on the tool box among stacks of boxes and bags of food. Holding the puppy, he nervously extended his license.

"Son, can you stand and step from the van?" the soldier requested.

"Sure." Perseus looked at Bobby then stepped out.

The soldier stepped into the van then immediately to the large tool chest. He lifted the lid. He places hi gun inside and it clanked against the tools. He shut the tool box. "Wow, this is a lot of Spam."

"Canned meat," Bobby corrected. "My father -in -law owns the Company. He hates it being called Spam."

Nodding, the soldier lifted the flap on a box then looked at another that sat alone on the floor by the tool chest. After peering in, he closed the flaps and finished looking all around the van and then stepped out. "OK, I'll let you go. Got to tell you though … buffalo flavored? I'm envious."

Bobby smiled. "Oh yeah." May I?" He pointed to the interior of the van.

"Sure."

Bobby stepped inside the van, grabbed a box he put in on the floor of the van, stepped out, and slid the box to the soldier. "Mixed flavors. Enjoy. You guys deserve it. Thank you for your service."

"You sure?"

"Yeah, we have plenty and we're going to his house now."

"That's really cool. Food of the Apocalypse." The soldier smiled and grabbed the box. "Be safe."

"We will. Thank you." Bobby flashed a quick smile.

Perseus walked to the van and stepped up, looking at Bobby as he did.

With the soldier gone, Bobby exhaled and widened his eyes. He closed the van doors and returned to the driver's seat.

"All good?" Brady asked.

"Perfect. I gave him a box of meat." Bobby started the van. "Your father …" He shifted the gear and moved forward as the sawhorse was removed to let them through. "He's a freaking genius. How the hell did he know that would work?"

"Ralph was an amateur magician. It's about creating the illusion."

"I'm just relieved." Bobby drove further down the road. When he knew they were clear, he called back to his brother. "Ok, it's clear."

Perseus reached for the box next to the tool chest, the same one the soldier had opened. "Good girl for not moving." He lifted the faux layer of canned ham, cans that were placed neatly on a piece of cardboard. "I know it's hot."

Sammy was curled tightly in a fetal position in the small space. "And heavy. It was heavy."

Perseus laughed. "You did great."

"I'll be better next time. I moved."

He lifted her to his lap. "Hopefully, we'll just get to Aunt Jean's and there won't be a next time."

New York, NY

What was Tom thinking?

So consumed with his grief, he just didn't want to go back home and then he ran out of gas. He swam in pain and poor Jenny felt it. She cried a lot as well.

Tom was a mess.

Then when they ran out of gas, there wasn't even an option to get more. He was just driving around, evading going home, and his SUV fluttered to a stop. Tom hadn't even noticed the gas gauge.

He had a back pack of food and he tossed that around his shoulder. Cars were parked in the middle of the road, some, like Tom's, were abandoned; Others waited in long lines of traffic. The setting sun and riot noise added a frightening aspect to Tom's journey. Random strangers and people screamed at him to get the child off the streets. They tossed cans and other items.

It was insane. Jenny was a child, a small child.

Her words of 'Daddy, I'm scared', prompted Tom to get off of the streets. If people were yelling and throwing things at them, who knew what they were capable of in their fear?

St. Patrick's Catholic Church was a beacon of light even if only the lights above the doors were on. Would those same doors be open? He doubted it but it was worth a shot. At the very least, he and Jenny would huddle near the church for safety.

With a prayer in his mind, Tom pulled at the door.

It opened. He sighed out in relief and, with Jenny cradled to his chest, he walked in the church. He didn't let the door slam. He guided it quietly closed.

Despite how hard Tom tried to be silent, he wasn't. His footsteps made a noise echoing across the huge, high ceiling church and Jenny's sniffles and whimpers added to that.

He hushed her soothingly and held her closer as he sought a pew to sit down. He had been walking for hours.

It was dark expect for a few lights that lit the crucifix above the altar and the Blessed Mother Statue to the right. The church offered a feeling of sanctuary even if only a little while. Sliding in the pew, he set Jenny down, knelt on the kneeler, and made the sign of the cross.

For his entire life, Tom would never say he was religious, only ritualistic. He'd go to church on Sundays with his wife and kids when he could. He never missed Mass on a holy day and his envelope was placed in the collection basket every week.

On paper, Tom was a good Catholic.

But in that church, Tom felt ashamed for never paying attention, never caring, and never believing. Now he believed and if there really was a God, Tom needed Him.

After prayer, Tom sat on the pew and placed Jenny's head on his legs. He'd let her sleep and rest and after a while Tom would slip out when it was light.

That was the plan.

Just as he lifted a bottle of water from his bag, he heard the latching of locks. It came from behind him and then a creak and footsteps.

Tom closed his eyes tightly, hoping he wouldn't be seen, but the footsteps drew closer.

He felt another wave of crying building up and he fought it. He couldn't take having to leave. He couldn't put his daughter through anymore.

Tom felt the presence of the person was in the aisle beside him and finally looked up.

The priest was in his mid -forties, dark hair but speckled gray like Tom's. He gave a sad smile to Tom, genuflected, and then slid in the pew next to him.

"I've locked the doors for the night," the priest said.

"I understand."

Then he placed a hand over Tom's. "What brings you here so late?"

160

Tom's jaw tensed and a tightness hit his throat. He tried to speak, but couldn't. Words were hard. "I um …" He cleared his throat then spoke softly with weakened words. "I was out with my daughter. We ran out of gas. I was looking for something … anything right now. I don't know."

"Does she have the sickness?"

Tom shook his head and whimpered out a 'no'. He shook his head. "She's all I have, Father. All I have. I am so lost right now. I'm not doing right by her." Tom swung his head over to look at the priest. "I'm not. I'm a mess."

"You brought her here. That's not wrong."

Tom frowned. He tried not to but it was difficult. "My wife died yesterday. I never even went to find out what they did with her. I just wanted to protect what I had left. My son … He was shot, you know. They thought he was running because he was infected but he was running to me … to me." Tom lowered his head. "I want to say I buried my only son today. I didn't bury him. I left him at mass grave with thousands of others. No one would take him. No one would bury my son. What horrible atrocity could he have down that no one would bury him?"

Shoulders heaving, Tom cried.

"I'm sorry," the priest said. "I am so sorry."

"I was just driving. Not thinking. We ran out of gas. I didn't want to go home. It hurts to go there. And we had to walk. People were screaming at us, throwing things as if I held the disease myself. She's just a little girl."

"This whole thing is an abomination. I don't know and I won't try to guess what God's plan was in all this. Maybe He didn't cause this. Maybe He's trying to fix it and it's getting ahead of Him, but it makes no sense."

Tom took a moment and breathed out. "We'll leave. Can we just stay long enough to rest? I know you wanna lock up for the night."

"I do. But this is God's house, so it's your house. You are welcome here."

Fighting another wave of sadness, Tom just nodded.

"In fact, I … I'm alone here. I can use the help."

"Father?" Tom looked at him with question.

"Can you come with me? It'll be easier to show you. She'll be fine here. Trust me."

Tom looked down at Jenny. She had fallen asleep and, slightly apprehensive, Tom slid her from his lap and then rose from the pew after the priest.

The priest extended his hand. "Sam. My name is Sam."

"Tom." Tom shook his hand.

"This way." Sam turned and walked to the back of the church.

Priest or no priest, Tom was paranoid. What if it was a setup? What if the priest was taking him out? He thought that the whole journey through the back of the church, into the vestibule, and to a door that led down a darkened staircase. Just at the point when Tom started to really get concern, he heard it.

Voices.

Even laughter … children's laughter.

Sam paused at the big, wooden door and then opened it. "This is the only reason I haven't closed the doors of the church yet. I may have to soon."

Tom gasped when he looked inside what was probably the party hall of the church. The rented room for joyous occasions and family gatherings was now a place for displaced children. There had to be over fifty kids. They were mostly young with only a few older ones. They ate from paper cups and sat on the floor and in chairs. Some slept on blankets.

"I have two teenagers on the stage watching," Sam said. "You know, for the symptoms, so they can move the other children in case someone turns. But keeping the well together is the best option; together. We need to keep them together and away from the sick. It's not airborne. We know that."

"Where did they all come from?" Tom asked. "There are so many."

"Abandoned … parents. Their parents were scared and left them here. That's how I got the teenagers. They brought their siblings. A few, I found on these streets just wandering, left alone with nowhere to go. This is the state of humanity right now."

Tom swiped his hand over his mouth. "And you're by yourself."

"I am. I have sent the teenagers out to get food but I need help. You said you didn't want to go home. Maybe I can convince you to stay and help me out. We need to prepare for what's next. It's only going to get worse."

Tom chuckled emotionally. "How much worse can it get?"

"Oh," Sam gasped out emotionally. "Need you ask? Really? We went from a world denying the outbreak to fighting the outbreak. So quickly we went from fighters to runners. Children are now abandoned and treated like lepers. What's next is something I don't want to think about. These children are life's most precious commodity. I want to protect them. People are scared. They are now viewing children as a threat to mankind. Right now they are shunning them. How long will it take before people move it one step further?"

Tom didn't want to think about that step. His child was one of the marked, marked simply because she was a child.

Looking about the innocent faces, Tom knew what he had to do.

District 3

June 4 – Year 6 P.D.

Official Journal Entry of D3 Historian.

Day 2,372

We beat it. We survived the war. I received a message via Morse code that it was over. I was worried only briefly and, as I suspected, we weren't even touched because the theory has worked. In less than four years, the walls will no longer be needed, the electric charges will deplete, and the gates will open.

The future was secure. It will never be understood. The decision will never be accepted. But for the species to be continued, choices had to be made – just like I made the choice to be a volunteer. I was part of the call, part of the decision, the solution; and, it only goes to figure I had to be part of the Detaining.

Ten years of my life was nothing compared to what would have happened had the detaining not occurred.

There was more to it than anyone knew – so, much more. It was calculated. I informed the other D3 volunteers right away, but, except for my brother, they wanted nothing to do with me. He had no choice. The others … no one spoke to me until it was obvious that the food supply wasn't going to last the ten years then I was the answer again.

The feeling today after the Morse code message was so similar to the day we grew our first tomato.

I only found the location for the greenhouse. It was my brother who designed the perfect conditions and it was he who held that tomato in his hand, smiling from ear to ear, and saying "I'm a farmer. Damn, I am a farmer."

The volunteers basked in the growth and we knew we'd never go hungry.

The penthouse greenhouse was a sign that life would go on.

Today, the end of the war was another sign.

Life will prevail.

PART FOUR: HIDE AND SEEK

Curse of the Innocents

Blacon – Chester, England

October 17

One Month Later ...

Mary Proctor moved slowly. This was it for her, the end. She waited it out as long as she could until she saw no more movement on the street from her fifth floor flat.

She knew she was pushing it but what did she care. It was over. Done. Her two-bedroom flat was nothing but horrendous memories. Like most in her complex, she gave her all. She didn't do like a lot of parents. She didn't give up until she had to. She wasn't of the income level to afford a peaceful resolution for her children. She had to fight it, had to watch them suffer. They deteriorated before her eyes, going from rage filled animals to crying and innocent children.

How was she to make that decision? How was she to turn her back on them? She couldn't but now she didn't have a choice.

Three days earlier, helicopters flew overhead and dropped the leaflets. This was the day. The hour was near. Many left the complex as soon as the leaflets came, but not Mary. She actually debated on staying, not looking, and praying. But at the last second, with her children pounding at the bedroom door, banging and screaming, Mary made the choice.

She packed a small bag, placed her hand against the door, said her goodbyes, and expressed her love. Then Mary left the apartment.

No one else was leaving.

It had been silent in the area days before the leaflets were dropped. Blacon was the first area but it wouldn't be the last.

The percentage had been hit and it was time.

167

Because was the power was out, she took the stairs and left her darkened high rise.

The area was scattered with litter, mostly government flyers. She didn't want to look back, but after crossing the property, Mary stopped at the fence that surrounded the perimeter of the complex. She turned and looked back to her two-toned red and white high rise. Some windows were broken, some areas burned, but more frightening than all of that were the numerous red flags and shirts that hung from balconies and windows, the global symbol that the infected were there and the parents had given up.

Mary didn't see a need to hang a red flag.

No one was coming to get them or to help.

That stopped two weeks earlier.

She glanced down to the old watch she carried, said one more goodbye to the building, and walked through the open fence.

A car passed her at a high rate of speed. They beeped. It was warning to her to move, to walk faster.

Mary didn't. She kept her pace, kept walking and didn't look up when she heard the jets nearing. The high engine noise blared loudly and they zoomed overhead. Her entire being froze when she heard the firing of missiles. Seconds later, nothing but explosions rang out.

At that point, Mary turned around. There was no point in running as there was nowhere to go.

She should have stayed in her flat, at least that way she would have seen it coming. With a deep breath and closed eyes, she waited on the fireball that roared her way.

Chapter Seventeen

October 19

Washington DC

"I want to give up," Cyrus said, nearly in a whisper as he spoke on the phone with his brother.

"You cannot give up," Bobby said. "Why would you even say that?"

"I am on limited resources, power conservation, and no man power," Cyrus sighed out, looking about his lab. "I don't even know which way to turn or where to go next?"

"How about going back to control?"

"That's not an answer, Bobby, and you know it. It has to be beat or it has to burn out. Control is just a delay. We now know what are we delaying. These kids that are still alive and infected ... they ...they are surviving at minimum and eating just because their bodies say to. It's sad."

"What is DC like?"

"Quiet, not like New York or other cities. Very quiet. Many infected have been rounded up, but it's not helping what remains in the air and carried through bugs."

"What are they doing with the ones they ... rounded up?" Bobby asked.

Cyrus sighed out. "I don't know but I saw the camp. If they were my children, I'd want them to not suffer."

"You don't have a child, Cyrus, that's a lot easier said than done. For your niece, you have to keep trying."

Cyrus nodded then said, "I will. Thank you for taking a minute to talk to me."

"Anytime. Well, as long as there are still phones."

"Four hours a day."

169

Bobby chuckled. "It's something. Opus arrived finally. He got out of Boston."

"Have you left the farm?"

"Two weeks ago. The town was okay ... nothing much, a few flags. But we have to go out today. We need supplies and we're gonna barter some meat."

"Can you give me a progress report of the town when the phones are up tonight?"

"Will do."

"Take the light. I mean it."

"I will."

"Take care, big brother." Cyrus ended the call and just stared out.

Really, he was at a loss. He had tried everything imaginable but nothing worked. There was no way to turn around the infected and he had yet to stop the bacteria from its continuous path of damage. He really thought he had a breakthrough when he discovered that during an attack, the brain patterns were similar to seizures in epilepsy. But the infected children in the camp didn't respond to any anti -seizure medications, not like they did in the earlier cases of Nodding. There was, however, a level of photosensitivity in over ninety percent of the children in the infected camps. The effect of a strobe light or flashing red light triggered brief to mid -length absence seizures to full blown tonic-clonic seizures, instantly rendering the child immobile the second the light caught their attention. They either froze or dropped. But the seizure would only pause them enough for them to be taken. Afterward they always turned lucid and normal before cycling back into a Tantrum. Maybe the normalcy was nature's gift to a parent for one more moment with the child they were losing, a moment with the child they knew and loved and not the monster they became.

The photosensitivity wasn't a long term treatment. It couldn't be for the seizures it caused and triggered in excess could be deadly. Not to mention, Tantrum worsened because the brain suffered more damage.

Staring off in a state of his own self -doubt, Cyrus was surprised when his office lab door opened. There was no knock and the President walked in. President Henry Collingsworth walked in alone, no security, and it didn't appear as if anyone was with him at all. He was drawn, pale, and tired looking. He wore a tee -shirt and jeans, not typical presidential attire.

"Hey, Cyrus, how's it going?" he asked

"Henry?" Cyrus asked. "Are you … are you alone?"

"Yep. Walked out of the White House, got in a car and drove here. I don't have much staff and those I do have are needed to work on other things." He stepped closer. "You know why I'm here?"

Cyrus nodded.

"You, John, and General Blanding came up with it. I said I wouldn't move until I had the approval of all of you."

"I understand."

"Any progress?"

"No. We're still at a minimum … months maybe even years away."

"Can we sustain if we wait?"

Sadly, Cyrus peered at Henry. "At this rate, humanity is done." He shrugged. "In the UK they …"

"I don't care about the UK I don't care about any other country. Each is handling it their own way. We're behind. Everywhere else is rectifying the situation or trying to secure a future."

"In a much different way than us," Cyrus said. "We're being passive."

"Do you really want to be aggressive?" Henry asked. "Really? Because I don't; I have a child I have locked in a room to keep her safe. That's no way to live. I can't, with a good conscious, be the last sitting President and make the decision to erase the future. I cannot clean sweep. Your plan is a good one, drastic, but good. It could save the future for us."

"It could cause problems because as long as the U.S. still has the bacteria, we are still holding the threat to the world."

"We will face that when we need to. But right now, I have parents out there making the painful decision to have their child put out of their suffering. I have facilities humanely performing the procedure that have lines a block long," Henry huffed out emotionally. "I don't want another parent to have to make that choice. This has to end and the end begins with your final approval."

"I'm nobody. Make the call yourself."

"You're the brainchild of this." Henry shook his head. "We're all in or none in. We all will be affected by our decisions."

"We'll go down in history as the bad guys."

Henry shrugged. "I don't believe that. In the short term history, maybe, but ten years from now, ...no. We'll go down as the ones who took control. Tell me, Cyrus, so I can prepare emotionally as well."

"We hit the percentage. The threshold has been breached," Cyrus said softly. "It's time."

New York, NY

The abandoned emergency vehicles left randomly with lights flashing wouldn't last long. They were parked on the street to offer protection and a small security fort those trying to get to the supply trucks. Tom knew it would be short lived as he had already seen two cars destroyed. The older children were figuring it out and the light effect really had very little bearing on those older than twelve. The more dangerous ones were the hardest to control.

They were the ones shot on sight. They were not taken into custody, bound, or placed in a 'Peace' center. They were just killed, tossed in a truck, and burned.

These same children were probably loved and mourned before they died. What a desecration of society, Tom thought. But he was no better. On the street, Tom had to view them, not as children, but as 'things' because survival was difficult if he looked at them as children.

It wasn't just his survival now. He had Jenny and the other children living at the church and Father Sam. They had received over a hundred children and food dwindled fast. They had only a few incidents of 'turning' and no deaths. The most recent turns came from a group of children that arrived late and Tom figured they had probably already been exposed, so they kept them separate.

Upon the urging of Father Sam, Tom did not mention the number of children they had when he went every other day to the military trucks. He walked to all three food supply stations to get all that he could. Power was irregular and when it came on they took advantage of it. But in the last month, a few days with power was more normal than a few days without.

The church still had a good supply of candles and they used the drippings to create more. The number one thing Tom worried about was water. He stockpiled that at every chance picking up every bottle of water that he'd find. Immediately they started filling up cans and containers in case the water supply did stop.

It would. Tom was sure of it. They picked up a local radio station where the disc jockey, Red Rob, was communicating with others via a ham radio. He informed people in New York what was going on off the island.

He reported differently than the FEMA station.

Red Rob was pretty confident that the water was only left on and running by the Government until they wanted to close the cities.

FEMA said they would keep it going until the crisis was over.

Red Rob indicated a month or so, maybe three tops, and all would change. The U.K. was cleaning house of the infected, no matter how hard, to make way for a clean and infection clear next generation. They placed a ban on childbirth for at least a year.

The U.S., however, was doing things differently. According to Red Rob, the twenty cities weren't evacuated because of infection. They were evacuated for a plan. Five of them were being deconstructed and reconstructed for Detention Centers while the rest were being stockpiled as Renewal Cities for people to go, start anew, mourn, and wait. The government was focusing on rebuilding life through these cities.

It was inconceivable to Tom. How was the population of America going to fit into fifteen cities? Then again, the population had dwindled. For every child infected, at least one adult died. Tom supposed that the four million population of the U.S. was maybe half, if that. It was hard to say. They stopped giving numbers.

Father Sam and Tom listened nightly to Red Rob. Sam believed him and held faith in every word but Tom was skeptical. The newsman in him had to be that way.

Sam's unshakeable confidence in Red Rob's information came when he reported about Peace Centers opening up in fire stations, church's hospitals, and med fast centers. FEMA denied it until the beginning of October, and then they confirmed it. FEMA called them Option Centers. Tom and Sam like 'Peace' better.

"He's telling the truth," Sam said. "The government will admit it all soon. Wait and see."

Because of that, Tom couldn't take a chance of Red Rob being wrong about the water, so daily Tom snuck out, walked a block down the street, and filled three, five-gallon canvas water bags. They were heavy, topping over a hundred pounds, so he couldn't carry more. Even the five sided hydrant wrench wasn't light. That was how he got the water.

On this particular day, he could hear the children going through Tantrum – breaking glass, screaming, and yelling gibberish. The lone police car had one flashing light. That car was twenty feet from Tom and before it stood a child of six, fixated on the light, frozen in an induced seizure.

Filling the third bag, Tom heard the commotion grow closer. As it was just about filled, he raised his eyes to see three children racing down the street. They screamed madly at the top of their lungs as they apparently focused on Tom.

Fill, damn it, fill. Tom thought.

Done!

He grabbed the hydrant wrench. They were close, too close. He could run for it but not with the water. He didn't want to leave the water behind or the hydrant on. The healthy children needed it. Jenny needed it.

Catch the light, catch the lights ... come on!

He placed the wrench on the stem nut to shut off the water.

One child caught the lights, then two ... the third kept coming closer and closer.

The hydrant was off and Tom retracted the wrench. Just as he stood up, a child of about ten was right there. He cried out a scream at Tom and jumped. One bite, one scratch, or even saliva and Tom was done – doomed. Jenny would be alone.

Instinctively, Tom reacted and swung out the hydrant wrench, connecting with the child's torso. The moment he hit him, an instant heartbreaking pain struck Tom's gut.

That could have been Jerrod.

The boy sailed back, landed on the concrete, rolled over, and stood back up.

175

No. No. Tom shook his head whimpering the words. "Stay back. Please."

As if he weren't hurt or feeling anything, the boy came at Tom again.

"I'm sorry. I'm so sorry." Tom swung the wrench just one more time. This time it rendered the child motionless. Whether he killed the boy or knocked him out, it didn't matter. Tom was devastated by what he did. He was just a child, unaware and not in control. A child who didn't deserve the death sentence nature had handed him or what Tom had done to him.

Tom would never forgive himself. It didn't get easier. It wasn't the first child Tom had to put down in self-defense. It wouldn't be the last. When would it end? When would the madness stop? It was too painful. He felt for the child and the child's parents. He dropped the wrench, dropped to his knees, stared at the child, and cried.

Boardman, OH

Aunt Jean's farm sat eighteen miles southwest of the small highway town. It wasn't really a farm for growing food, not any more. After her husband died, she used the money to keep two hands under her employ to do the maintenance. Like her nephew Ralph, Jean made her money from other outlets. The farm was an escape and, as the Tantrum crisis grew, it was Brady's escape. With its acres of land and a long hidden driveway, it was the perfect place to keep Sammy secluded from other children.

Brady tried to secure her daughter between her legs on the floor and to pull her hair back in a ponytail. Sammy kept playing with her puppy, laughing and giggling, pulling on the too big homemade leash that had a heart on it.

176

"Sammy, sit still, please," Brady told her.

"Let the child be," Aunt Jean said. She sat in the chair, her walker to the side. She was older, in her eighties, and of good mind but her legs were weak as well as her bladder. Howard, her caretaker, had just brought her a cup of tea. The robust man in his thirties, once a factory worker, received his Certified Nursing Assistant certificate when that was the only field in which he could secure a job. He enjoyed it though and was good and caring with the elderly. When Jean hired him, he moved into the house when his wife took off with their children a week earlier. He had no idea where they went or if they were fine. He told Brady that being around Sammy helped. He tried, but every once and a while his mood shifted to a down one.

Brady understood.

"You know," Howard told her, "If you start at the ends and then move to the top of the head, you'll get the tangles better without the fussing."

"That's a great suggestion," Brady smiled.

"Here's another one," Aunt Jean added "Put down the brush and quit fussin' over the baby. Let her play with the dog. That's all she got to do."

"I want to take George outside and run!" Sammy said. "Please, Mommy. Please. He wants to run with me."

"Okay, let me get my shoes on." Brady placed down the brush.

"If you don't mind," Howard said. "I'll take her out. I need a laugh and Opus is chopping wood."

Aunt Jean snorted a laugh. "Sorry." She snorted again. "The Good Lord, help us if we got to rely on Opus to protect us."

"Aw." Brady shook her head. "Be nice. Opus is a nice guy. He's trying." She grabbed on to Sammy's hand. "Wait. Give me a kiss. I'll be right out."

Sammy did. After darting a kiss to her mother, she locked hands with Howard and, with the puppy in her other arm, left.

"You okay?" Jean asked Brady.

"Yeah, I'm fine." Brady proceeded to tie her shoe. "I'm just worried about Bobby, Perseus, and Dad."

"They'll be fine."

"You heard Howard. Boardman isn't the same."

"They'll be fine," Jean repeated. "Three men can handle themselves."

Brady nodded and stood. "I'm going to go out."

"Good, the fresh air will help. Take a sweater. Bray ... can you turn on the old radio, just in case that man comes on the off station?"

"Sure, thing, Aunt Jean." Brady turned on the radio as she passed it. She knew who Jean was talking about, but Brady didn't put stock into his outlandish accusations. She took stock in what Cyrus said. After all, Cyrus was in the thick of it all.

Outside, the puppy ran circles around Sammy, the sound of Opus slamming the ax filled the air, and Howard stood off to the side watching Sammy while smoking a cigarette. He was also looking at his phone.

"Hey," Brady stood next to him. "Whacha doing? Do you have a signal?"

"Nah, just habit and wishful thinking." Howard replied. "I wish my phone was charged so I could see a picture of my kids. All those times I said I was gonna take this phone to Wal-Mart and make prints. Never did. Makes you wonder how many parents are thinking like me right now."

"A lot, I can tell you." Brady rubbed the chill from her arms. "It's getting cold."

"Hence ... why Opus is chopping wood," Howard pointed out. "Hard to believe so much bad is happening when we have such a beautiful fall day like this."

"I know. Howard ..." She waited for him to look at her. "What do you make of this all? We haven't talked."

"Breaks my heart," Howard said and hit his cigarette. "What did these kids do to be the targets of something so vicious? I

178

remember reading about this infection years and years ago. It's here and mightier than ever."

"Do you think your kids will make it through?"

"To what?" Howard asked. "Through until the threat has passed? Who knows if that's possible? This isn't the end of the world; but it could be the end of Man's time."

"I keep looking at Sammy. I'm so glad she's at a safe age, but … I don't know what I would do if she was infected."

"If my kids were infected …. I'd opt out."

Brady looked at him curiously.

He continued. "I'd take them to a center and let them have their peace. Then I'd opt out. But since I don't know where and how my kids are … I have to keep going."

"I don't know if I could be that brave. I think I'd hold out for a cure."

Howard glanced at her and said, "They may beat this. They may stop this. But once it hits, there's no way to undo the damage. Sort of like throwing acid on a sponge, it eats away the brain. You can't and it can't be brought back. Saving your kid is condemning them. So you save them for who? Them or you? Have you seen an infected kid, Brady?"

"One. One boy. He was very violent."

"I've seen them when they weren't in them episodes. Those violent episodes happen a few times during the day. For the most part, they are emotionless. They meander, cry. They don't know you and only have a few specks of clarity. It's sad. They don't eat right, so they are dying a slow death." Howard finished his cigarette and tossed it. "Makes me sick."

"Bobby doesn't really like talking about this so thank you."

Howard nodded.

"What about what that crazy radio guy said about them taking all the kids, sick or not?" Brady asked.

"You got your brother-in-law telling you that's a lie so why worry."

Brady lowered her head. "I do. Don't you."

179

"I'd rather have my kids locked up, safe and alive than at risk of illness."

"But they aren't seeing kids as kids. They are seeing them as…I don't know…monsters. Risks?"

"Who's they?" Howard asked. "The government, the World? A lot of places are handling this differently."

"Yeah, they're killing kids and that's wrong."

"Yeah it is. Then again, I'm a parent and I'm looking at it from a parent's point of view, I want to save the kids. But in the big picture, we have to save the race." His head cocked when George the puppy started yapping. "They aren't killing the kids. They're killing the infection that is threatening everyone else."

"Same difference;"

"No, for example, let's say eighty percent of dogs and cats carried an illness that could render man extinct. What would you do?"

"It's different. They're animals."

"They are carriers. A carrier is a carrier."

Brady shook her head. "I don't want to live in a world that disregards children so easily."

"Neither do I. But those of us with small children are only a fraction of the population. There's a whole bigger fraction without kids. They see this differently. They see this as a fight to stay alive. The infection kills adults. Kills them."

"Why not just let it run its course?" Brady asked. "Why not just wait. Hide out and wait."

"No matter how strongly we feel about actions against children, something has to be done. Like it or not, man can't be extinct. If we allow it, then we are being selfish. If we do nothing, we are aiding extinction."

"I don't believe that. I don't believe we are really facing extinction with it."

"Then you are naïve. If we don't cure it or find a way to evade it then we're done. Our children are our future," Howard said. "If we allow something so fierce to wipe out our young then we are all but erasing that future."

Two weeks earlier, the trading post and military distribution was just two blocks from the McDonald's located in the strip mall with the large discount department store. Two weeks earlier was how long it was since Bobby and Perseus had been in town.

Ralph never was there, he came straight from his home with a huge stockpile of canned meat.

On this day, though, everything was different. The few flags hanging from windows turned into multiples and remnants of horrific fires were smoldering. There were no cars on the road and when they pulled into the strip mall, there were bodies. Bodies everywhere. There was also a military distribution truck, but soldiers lay dead near it.

It was apparent by the bodies they had died from infection. They were wretched.

Wretched, twisted, with puddles of fluids by their mouths. Something occurred while everyone was there. But worse than the sight of the bodies were the multitudes of children just moving aimlessly and slowly. They didn't look at Bobby's van or move out of the way.

It was as if Bobby's van wasn't even there.

A few cried, sat on the ground and cried but no one attacked. For the most part, they just wandered.

To Bobby, there was a weird and eerie feeling in the air. "Anyone else feel like they are in the Hitchcock movie, *The Birds*?" he asked.

"Don't know that movie," Perseus said.

"I do," Ralph replied. "Right before they attacked, the birds just hung around. Yeah." He peered out the window. "I understand exactly what you're saying."

"We still need dry goods and aspirin for Aunt Jean," Bobby said, driving slowly. "I'll pull up as close as I can but I'm not hitting these kids."

Ralph nodded.

Bobby drove. The closest he could get to the front of the store was about twenty feet. There were too many kids. He turned the van, backed up as cautiously as he could and, leaving it running, he placed it in park. "All right, since we ain't trading, Ralph, I want you to sit here and get ready to drive. Perseus and I will go in the store. Do a quick grab."

"You got the light?" Ralph asked.

Perseus held up the handheld strobe light. "Ready."

"We may luck out," Bobby said. "Have them on a down cycle. They don't seem to be attacking or screaming, so we move slowly. Very slow." He waited until he got nods of agreement and slid from the driver's seat. He slipped to the back of the van and, once Ralph was in position, Bobby grabbed a canvas bag. He handed it to Perseus. "We stick together. We grab and go. Got it?"

"We ain't never done this before, Bobby," said Perseus. "In fact, we haven't been around infected kids. We don't know what we're doing."

"If you're worried, stay back," Bobby told him calmly.

"That's not it. I just don't know if this is all that good of an idea. We're going in blind."

Ralph asked. "How are supplies? Do we really need them right now? Maybe let's go back and get Howard. He's dealt with these kids."

Bobby nodded. "I know what you're saying, but how do we know when we come back they won't be in one of their violent episodes and then we have to go up against them. I don't want to hurt a kid, sick or not."

"I understand. You're right. Let's just do this," Perseus reached for the handle of the van's back door.

"Slow." Bobby said. "Try not to make a sound."

Perseus nodded his agreement then carefully and slowly pushed down the handle. Once it was down, he ever so slightly pushed open the back door.

It wasn't open but six inches when Perseus, with his hand still on the door, screamed loudly when a child pounced onto his arm and sunk his teeth deep into the flesh of Perseus' wrist.

Bobby quickly reacted. Using his foot, he pushed at the child. It took three shoves and the child released. After hurriedly shutting the van door, Bobby grabbed the first cloth he could find and wrapped it on Perseus' bleeding wound.

"Go. Go. Go," Bobby urged.

"I can't," Ralph said. "We're surrounded."

"I'm gonna die," Perseus said, hyperventilating. "I'm gonna die in a few minutes."

"No, you're not." Bobby looked at the bite. "It's not that bad. Ralph, go."

"I can't!" Ralph yelled.

"Cyrus said," Perseus breathed heavily. "He said. One bite, one scratch, you die."

Bobby cringed in pain and grabbed on to his brother. "I swear to you. You aren't dying. Ralph, go."

"Bobby, I just can't." Ralph shook his head. "They're all over. I am not running them down. I'm not. You wanna run them down. You do it. But I won't."

A few bangs against the van commenced, followed by screams from outside. Within seconds, the van was jolting. How many were out there? How many started attacking the van? Bobby peered at Ralph who had lowered his head in defeat against the steering wheel, and then Bobby pulled his baby brother into him.

Where would they go anyhow? There was no help to be found and no time anyhow. The violent episodes didn't last long, not from what Bobby heard. They'd wait and figure it out once things calmed down. But none of that mattered at that second to Bobby.

Perseus was bit. End of story.

"I'm scared. I don't wanna die," Perseus spoke weakly.

"It's okay. I have you. I have you." His heart raced and a pain filled his entire body as Bobby clung tight to Perseus. According to Cyrus, within minutes, the bacteria would attack and Perseus would convulse and then leave this world. But the minutes passed and nothing happened except more sadness from Perseus and increased tension and pain over the fear of the inevitable.

The attacks grew more intense outside and Bobby blocked out all the exterior commotion, focusing on Perseus, holding him, keeping eye contact, and savoring what moments he had left with his little brother.

Then something occurred. Amidst the loud commotion, Perseus grew still. He stopped moving and his head dropped against Bobby chest. Blood rushing to his ears, Bobby's heart sank and his body trembled. He brought his lips to his brother and that was when he realized Perseus had defied the odds. He hadn't died. He only passed out. At that moment, under attack or not, Bobby had to figure a way for them to get out. He had to get in touch with Cyrus. They may not have been out of the woods, and it may have been too late, but he had to tell his brother something was different. Perseus didn't die, and medically, that had to mean something.

Chapter Eighteen

Mon City, PA

In a world falling apart, Nola was glad she at least spoke to her brother. The last conversation was two days earlier.

"The city is still sealed," Tom said.

"We have this house, Tom. You can come here."

"I will. We will as soon as we're out."

"How is Jenny?" she asked.

"She's scared. Adjusting but healthy. Carlie? Ben? Eddie?"

"All ... all of them fine. Get here, Tom. We need to be together as a family."

And that was all that was said. Perhaps she should have been honest with her brother. All was not fine. She needed him. Every day she kept looking out the window in hopes he'd show up, but then the phone would ring and it would be Tom.

She'd stop looking for the night.

Nola was taking as what she called an emotional break. She needed it. She had just made it back from a food run. There were six jars of peanut butter on the shelf and she took them all. She also grabbed the last two cans of beef stew. A part of her felt guilty, but there wasn't anyone around.

The town was bare. So many had left and, with it being an older town, very few children were around.

She saw a few wanderers, but none attacked her. She was ready, though, in case they did. Food was rationed and she did the best she could. After a good cry, she washed her face. Then, using a Sterno, Nola heated up the can of beef stew. It would be a hearty meal served with crackers that were topped with peanut butter.

She picked up paper plates and after the brown thick substance bubbled, she placed a serving for each of them. Not too much for Ben and Carlie. They didn't eat much and lately, they were barely eating at all.

Eddie was in the dining room. As she carried his lunch, she paused when she heard the odd sound of it – the FEMA station interruption tone. FEMA electronic newscasters only broadcasted a few times a time and usually at the same times.

Lately it was the same message, *"If you or your loved ones are overwhelmed by the experience of the infection, the Option centers are available twenty-four hours a day. Please see local government installations for locations.'*

Nola heard that message so much she actually went to the Mon City Police department to see if there was a sign posted.

It listed several locations. Several locations? All of which were within miles of her new home. None of them were hospitals, but all were conveniently close to a field or factory.

For two weeks that was the only real message playing. The people, Nola included, were in the dark.

Typically after twelve, the airwaves were silent.

The tone then simple electronic message of, *"The President of the United States will address the nation today at Four P.M. Eastern Standard Time. Be advised, the President will address the nation."*

Pause.

Repeat.

Again.

The President was addressing the nation. Something was happening. Something was changing and Nola filled with hope. Maybe they found a cure. Maybe the madness was over.

She carried the plate into the dining room where Eddie was position near the window for light. He read what he always did. The Bible.

A young man who hadn't been in a church since his first Holy Communion read The Bible every day. He told Nola, if they make it, there was one reason.

He looked studious and in control, calmer than anyone Nola had encountered.

She set his plate before him. "Eat. I'll give you a little water after. We have to ration."

"Okay, thank you, Mom. Are you eating?"

"I will. I want to make sure Ben and Carlie eat."

"Mom ..."

"Eat." She pointed at the plate, then returned to the kitchen, and grabbed the two plates of food for Ben and Carlie. She carried them up the stairs and to the master bedroom. She gave that room to Ben and Carlie because oddly enough there were twin beds in there.

With her elbow, she knocked on the door and called out, "Lunch, babies." After balancing the plates on one arm, she opened the door.

Ben was half asleep. He sat on the floor between the bed and the wall. Nola smiled at him. "You hungry?"

No sooner did she ask, and not surprising her, she heard the fast unraveling of a chain and Carlie raced from the other side of the room, stopping cold when the chain ran out and she snarled madly, her head shaking back and forth.

Carlie's long hair was matted, Nola had tried to brush it the day before while Carlie was in a calm stage but it tangled right back.

Her face looked paler than it did the day before, but Nola attributed that to the fact Carlie wasn't eating like Ben. Ben only had a couple of Tantrum episodes a day, where Carlie was different. She raged a lot and then snapped from that to a drone - like state to lucid and crying.

Ben was still restrained by a long piece of fabric Nola found in Mrs. Rogers' sewing room, but Carlie chewed through her restraints in three days and Nola had to get the chain.

It was the one and only time she used the light method on Carlie.

Both children, however, were also restrained by old shirts tied around them like straightjackets. That was Eddie's idea. With their arms restrained, there was no fear of scratches.

"Sweetie, Mommy's gonna feed your brother," Nola told Carlie.

Carlie snapped, her head went back and forth and Nola set the food on the bed.

She lifted a pair of gardening gloves, put them on, and crouched before Ben. She ran her hand down his face, then leaned forward and kissed him. The gloves protected her fingers from a bite.

Ben didn't make eye contact. Then as she had done every day, twice a day, for nearly three weeks, Nola fed Ben. She opened his mouth, inserted the food, and held his mouth closed until Ben chewed and eventually swallowed.

She squirted water in their mouth using a water bottle. That was the best she could do. She'd attempt to feed Carlie next. Hopefully by the time she was done with Ben, Carlie would calm. She usually did.

Nola gave a calm, unfazed appearance but the truth was Nola was far from calm and unfazed. She was dying inside, tormented, and beaten. She trudged on daily, taking care of her children, because sick or not, she was their mother.

She loved them regardless and would do all that she could. She held out hope.

To her, there really was no other choice.

New York, NY

"Daddy!" Jenny cried out when Tom arrived. She raced down the center aisle of the church, throwing her arms around Tom's legs.

"Daddy's sorry he took so long, sweetie." Tom crouched down and embraced his daughter.

"I was scared for you."

"I know. I'm sorry." He held tight then lifted his head when Sam walked toward him.

"You look beaten," Sam said.

"I am." Slowly, Tom stood, still keeping his hand on Jenny. He felt beaten both emotionally and physically. His body hurt all over. He hadn't bathed properly in a long time and his skin itched along with his head. Sam didn't look much better.

"Everything okay out there?" Sam asked.

"Nothing will ever be okay out there. How about here?"

Sam lowered his head.

"What?" Tom questioned. "What now."

Sam shifted his eyes to Jenny then to Tom. "We had another Lawson child turn."

Biting his lip, Tom turned his head and twitched it in disgust. "Doesn't matter what we do. When will they stop getting infected?"

"I don't know."

"Where is he?"

"Dressing room behind the altar, we got everyone else out before he touched them."

Tom nodded and exhaled. "You have everything ready?"

"We don't have to do this now."

"Now or later … does it really matter anymore?" Tom asked. "Let's do this now before it gets too late."

Jenny looked up at her father. "Please stop going out there, Daddy. Please."

"Baby, someone has to. We need water and the kids that get sick need help. I'll be careful. The helping place is right up the street."

After running his hand down her head, he kissed her and followed Father Sam to the back of the church.

One of the teenagers stood by the door. He extended the hand-held light to Tom. "He's quiet in there now. "

"When did he go Tantrum last?" Tom questioned.

Sam answered. "He hasn't. He went straight into the staring state."

"Just in case." Tom prepped the light. "Be ready."

Sam held up the long white garment. Tom knew they'd use that to restraint the child. There was only one Lawson child left, Jason. He was eleven. Tom knew a child of that age had to be controlled or taking him for help wouldn't be easy.

"On my call," Tom said.

The teenager grabbed the door handle.

Tom lifted the light. "One … two … three … now."

The teenager flung the door open and Tom flicked on the light.

Jason ran toward Tom but stopped. He froze and locked on the light. After a moment, his arms dropped. Another thirty seconds and Jason dropped to the floor. His left leg jerked a little and his head twitched in tiny little movements.

"We got about a minute," Tom hurried to Jason. "Let's get him secure."

Sam placed the white robe around the boy, securing it against him, and restraining the movement of his arms. Tom was right. The child woke but he wasn't violent or lucid He just stared.

"I hate this shit." Tom lifted the boy to his feet. "We'll go out the back."

"Tom," Sam called to him. "You don't need to do this now. The President is coming on to make a speech."

"I don't care." Tom shook his head leading Jason. It was rough because the child barely moved.

"You all right?" Sam asked.

Tom paused at the door with Jason. "No. I'm a child killer, Sam. How horrible is that?"

"You're doing what you need to do, Tom. God forgives you."

"Yeah, well, I appreciate it, but I can't forgive myself." With his head a little lower, Tom escorted Jason out of the back room, down the hall and, eventually, he had to lift him and carry him out.

The Center was only a block away and Tom stopped a few times to get a breather. Jason was heavy. Though not very weighted, he was tall and hard to carry.

It was a light day at the Center. Typically at the church they could hear people in line crying, or children screaming. Some even stopped by to pray afterward. Two days earlier, Tom had to wait in line, a long line that was nearly a block long.

It was the worst day he experienced there. He had been there a lot. But that day, so many parents wept. So many kids were lucid and that made things worse. It reminded Tom of the day he dropped off Jerrod at the mass burial. In a sense, it was the same thing.

There wasn't a line, not really. Bill Haynes was there. He was a soldier who worked the streets and found children, sort of like the dog catcher of the city. There were several only they didn't catch dogs.

Just as he walked through the door, a huge truck rolled by and a lump formed in Tom's throat. All those bodies … all those children.

It didn't get easier. He wasn't as desensitized as he hoped he'd get. It affected him worse every single time.

From behind the desk at the former community recreation center, the familiar face of Janelle offered a tired smile. She wore light blue scrubs, her dark hair was pulled back, and a few strands dangled in her face.

NODDING – JACQUELINE DRUGA

"Hey, Tom," she said tiredly. "How's it going?"

"Eh." Tom grunted.

Another compassionate smile and she lifted a clipboard to the counter.

Tom knew the routine. Janelle was the one that explained it all the first time he arrived there.

"I'm sorry," she said to him that first day. *"I know this is difficult,"*

"This isn't my child," Tom told her.

"Still it's hard. I know."

He didn't understand at first why the Option Center wasn't at a hospital. Some were, but they found places like the YMCA and others centers to convert solely for parents who took the Option or strangers, like Tom, who found an infected child.

When out of curiosity he asked how it worked, did the kids suffer, Janelle explained she never watched the 'finishing' but was certain the kids didn't suffer.

They were taken to a sealed room with happy pictures on the walls and toys all around, like a playroom. Most children were in a drone state when placed there because if they were violent the photosensitivity method usually calmed them. Once in a while a child was in a lucid state and Janelle said it made it hard for everyone, not just the parents.

The parents would take one last look through the window and then leave. No one really watched their child leave the earth.

Released from restraints, the child or children, depending how many were waiting, were placed in the room among all the happy items.

The gas was then released. It was done in moments.

It didn't matter how they did it; to Tom it was a twisted Mary Poppins version of the concentration camps. It was disturbing. Society was wrong for doing it.

Tom was just as guilty. He was dropping them off.

Once Janelle told him, Tom had only seen the ones that were recently infected. The children who had been infected weeks and months were ill. It was sad and they were suffering. She saw it on their faces and their skin. Some kids were found still restrained at the home, abandoned with a red flag or their parents dead. It was inhumane. It was humane.

Was that her reasoning? Was she convincing Tom that day or herself?

Why call it an Option Center, because there was no other Option. There were no hospitals to take them or facilities to care for the sick just ... euthanizing.... Euthanizing.

Tom signed the paper after filling it out. What was the use? Was someone actually keeping track somewhere? It was the twelfth time he dropped someone off.

A man in a thick bio suit walked up and took Jason. He was gentle. It didn't make it any easier. Tom said goodbye to the boy he had only known a week or so and, as he always did, he apologized to him as well.

Janelle laid her hand over Tom's as she reached for the clipboard. "Every day there are less and less. It'll end soon. It'll be over soon. I feel it."

"I hope." Tom gave a single nod and turned.

"Tom."

Tom stopped walking. "Yeah."

"The President is coming on. Maybe he'll say something positive."

Tom shook his head. "I don't think there's anything the President can say that will make a difference. Have good one." On that, he turned and kept on walking.

Washington, DC

Perseus had been bitten.

193

That was all Cyrus heard and his entire being crumbled. His heart beat faster, blood rushed to his ears, and he was filled with an immediate sense of painful grief; his little brother, his baby brother.

Then Bobby told him something else. Perseus hadn't gotten ill. He had no reaction whatsoever. In fact, he was fine.

Cyrus breathed out a deep sigh of relief. It wasn't the first time he had heard of someone surviving a bite. Children too young to catch the infection didn't get sick – that was if they survived the attack of another child. Seven adults to date had been bitten or scratched and showed no signs.

Those seven adults were moved to a secure facility for testing, research, and possibly a link to a cure.

Perseus would have to go as well.

But unlike the others, Perseus would have to wait. Too much was going to happen over the next ten days. Final plans were in motion and Cyrus had to make sure where he was going first before he determined where they'd put his brother.

If anyone was going to be working on and testing Perseus, it would be Cyrus.

Cyrus was the Government's man on the project, but there were private facilities working around the clock. They shared information including those bitten and not infected.

Cyrus would keep the information about Perseus quiet.

Cyrus told Bobby he'd get back to him and to keep giving Perseus antibiotics. He urged his brother to listen to the President's message and then he apologized.

He was pretty certain Bobby didn't know why or even ask why he was getting an apology.

Bobby would know soon enough.

It was over. It was done. The grim reaper of reality knocked on the door and humanity answered. The time was at hand for desperate measures and the U.S. was taking a completely different approach.

The shared data and information was bleak.

194

In the US, before the infection, there were close to sixty million children under the age of fifteen. One third of those wouldn't be touched by Tantrum. Yet, if half of them were alive, the world was lucky. They had fallen victim to the attacks as did the adults.

By body count alone, half the children were infected or dead.

That was the amount accounted for.

Cyrus believed they were lucky if twenty percent of the youth population was alive and healthy. Half of them faced infection.

Without the young, there was no future.

The adults were fading just as fast —by suicide, attacks, and infection.

The madness had to stop and, as Cyrus looked at his watch, he knew in less than an hour the movement to gain control of man's survival would be underway.

It was the most drastic measure that could be taken. No one was going to like it. However, what choice did anyone have, especially when the alternative was extinction?

Chapter Nineteen

The Speech

Mon City, PA

It is a sad, no wait ..., the saddest day of all when we as a people must make decisions to secure our future and the decisions are...handle our most precious commodity. But isn't life a precious commodity. If there is no one left, then life does not go on.

Nola heard it, but she knew none of what the President said. The main reason for his speech didn't apply to her.

The speech took less than ten minutes and Nola heard all she needed to hear. She wanted to hear the speech. Perhaps that was why she took drastic measures to get some peace and quiet, a break, maybe even close her eyes to sleep since Nola hadn't slept well since the children were infected.

Placing two tablespoons of Benadryl in a medicinal syringe, she opened Ben and Carlie's mouths, injected the medicine, and held their mouths closed until they swallowed.

It didn't knock them out completely, but it made them sluggish. She posted a note on the Tasty Twist window letting others know that it worked. Everyone posted notes there; how to restrain, how to feed ... everything. Every parent struggling was sharing what they could.

The Option Centers will close on November first. Following the closing of the Option Centers, parents caring for their infected children will have two weeks to hang the red flag. These

196

children will be handled humanely during the clean sweep period. Parents not choosing the Option Center or red flag after the clean sweep ... they, and their children, are on their own.

How does a parent make that choice, Nola wondered. Every day she looked at her children and they were still the light of her life. She loved them without prejudice. How does a mother or father make the decision to place their child at peace? She couldn't do it, not at that moment.

On her own how would she manage? Could she?

As in every war there comes a time to forge ahead in victory and there comes a time to cut all loses and retreat. We are not winning this war. We are not even close. It is time, in order to ensure the continuity of the human race, we must retreat. We are asking all those over the age of sixteen, healthy and able -bodied to retreat west to renewal cities. Mass transportation will be provided in a list of cities that will be read following this speech. Beginning November first, all Government resources will be focused on these western cities. No longer will there be water trucks, supply trucks, or military presence. Any individuals choosing to stay behind and not reside in the renewal cities will be left to their own resources. We must focus on one area to rebuild, to protect, and make sure that life does go on.

"What does this mean, Mom?" Eddie asked, as he listened. "What does this mean?"

Nola shook her head.

"The renewal cities? Able bodied? That does that mean I can't go?" Eddie sounded panicked.

"Eddie ..."

"How we going to do this? The babies are sick. We are going to be left behind. Do you know what this world will get like?"

"I have a feeling, yes." Nola turned to him. "Eddie, I have taken care of you and loved you since the second you were born. I have no intention whatsoever of not taking care of you now. I'll figure out a way. I figured out the wheelchair, right? I'll figure it out." She grasped his hand.

"So basically, if you aren't over sixteen and you aren't healthy, then you're screwed."

Nola shook her head. "Not screwed. Just gonna have an uphill battle. Survival isn't being in a renewal city. It's beating this one way or another. We haven't had an easy life. I think that was God's way of preparing us for a rough time in the future. We may be abandoned here soon." Nola leaned forward and kissed him. "But we are not done. Not yet."

Boardman, OH

"No!" Brady emotionally cried out.

Ralph, at a loss and in shock, ran his hand down his face. "Jesus. This isn't happening."

"It is," Bobby said strongly, "and we all need to calm down."

Opus shook his head. "How? How do we calm down?"

Perseus spoke up. "Our brother is in this. Cyrus is there. We're good. I wouldn't worry."

"I would," Aunt Jean said. "This is out of your brother's hands."

Brady whimpered out another, "No. I have to get Sammy."

Bobby grabbed her arm, pulling her back. "Let her nap. Nothing is happening now."

The President's speech.

Everything was surreal and it almost seemed as if they were listening to a fictional radio show. It was inconceivable.

In order to create an environment conducive to subjugate the infection, children will be segregated by age. As of 3:30 p.m. today, an executive order, enforced by remaining Congress, has been enacted into law making it mandatory for all parents and caretakers of healthy uninfected children, fifteen years of age and younger to surrender these children to the Government.

When Brady heard the President utter those words, she was speechless. Gasps erupted and Bobby gave a 'shush'.

They had waded through everything else.

Surrender the children.

For the last six weeks, designated cities have been prepped to handle the segregation and isolation. They will continue to be prepared for long term use. Every precaution will be used to prevent infection in the city. The detaining of the young will remain in effect for a period of no longer than ten years and no shorter than such a time four years has passed since civilization has seen the last infected.

Surrender the children.

The cities will be manned with staff and volunteers, along with military personnel, to ensure safety and wellbeing. No contact will be made with those inside the Detaining Districts. No one gets in. No one gets out.

This is mandatory. On November first, a clean sweep will commence. Door to door sweep of the cities and rural areas to ensure all children have been surrendered. It is in your best interest and the best interest of your child and humanity to surrender the children. While we conceivably cannot find every child, those who are outside the renewal cities and Districts will be left without medical resources, food, and or protection.

Raging from the living room where they gathered around the radio, Brady sought out her daughter. Sammy, so tiny, was cuddled in bed with George, on top of the covers with a blanket over them both.

She swept the sleeping child into her arms. When she did, Ralph and Bobby walked in the room.

"I can't do it," she said. "I can't give her up. I can't put a three year old in the hands of the Government for ten years. She's a baby. I can't give her up. We tried so hard for her."

"We don't need to," Ralph said. "We have all the resources we need right here. We'll make it secure. We hide out here. Screw the renewal cities. Bet lots of folks take that attitude. You heard them. Rural and cities. They'll never check here."

"If they do," Bobby said. "We'll hide her. She's not going anywhere."

Brady pressed her lips tighter to Sammy. "Promise? I won't be able to handle it. I'll die. What will she think? She'll think we abandoned her. Oh God."

Bobby shook his head. "She will not be without us." He placed his hand on Brady's face. "I will not surrender our daughter."

And the President's final words ever spoken to the nation
….

200

Though it is small consolation, we are battling this infection. We are fighting every day and will not stop, no matter how long it takes. We will beat this. Maybe not today, maybe not next year, but we will, and along with the measures we have taken, though extreme, this will become a painful page in our history books, not an end to history all together.

New York, NY

Tom had stopped at another hydrant to wash up before returning to the church. When he did, he noticed the window to the pharmacy had been broken. He never wanted to break a window, so he never went into the locked store.

He knew what he wanted, candy for the kids or some sort of treat. He carefully stepped through the broken window, steering clear of the jagged glass. The candy would be out front, he was certain, but as soon as he stepped into the store, he saw a trail of empty peanut butter cup wrappers. Someone had the same idea. It had to have been a child. Not knowing if it was an infected one, Tom didn't take a chance. He grabbed as much candy as he could and left the store.

He was cold. The weather had definitely switched up and he picked up the pace to the church.

Slipping inside the doors, he felt a sense that something was wrong especially when he walked into the main church and the children were all seated in pews while Father Sam was kneeling at the altar facing, the large crucifix that hung from the ceiling.

His hands were folded.

Had someone died?

He exhaled a heavy gasp of relief when he heard Jenny whisper, "Daddy" and then Tom walked to the altar.

"Sam?" he called. "What's going on?"

Sam made the sign of the cross and only turned his head to Tom. "You missed the President's speech."

"What the hell did he say?"

"It's called 'The Detaining'. All healthy children are to be surrendered to the Government and locked up until the infection has run its course. They're saying years. Everyone else is to go west. My guess everything in the middle will be a wasteland and people will be left to fend for themselves."

"Wait. Wait. Surrender the kids?"

Sam nodded.

"Not happening."

"But they said they'll do a clean sweep of the area …"

"Not happening," Tom was adamant. "They aren't taking all I have left and hiding her for years. Taking her and I'll never know if she is well or sick, lives or dies. No."

"But what choice do we have?" Sam asked. "They will go door to door."

"So we do all we can. I'll go tomorrow and if I have to be out all day, I will. I'll get supplies. We ration, we buckle down, we hide, and we don't let them in."

"Should we?"

"Damn right we should," Tom stated strongly. "I am not giving up my child or any of these children. Not easily and not without a fight. There is no surrender on my part. That's not an option."

Washington, DC

Henry Collingsworth made the final address to the nation from his desk in the bare Oval Office. To preserve what they could, everything was taken to the bunkers below and sealed.

The knock on the door jolted him. It was one of very few remaining.

"The plane is ready sir. We have to leave," the aide said.

"The General?"

"He's ready to move once you're gone and safe," the aide replied. "We still have many men and women willing to do what they need to do to keep this country alive. They'll man the Detaining Stations."

"The message is playing now?" Henry asked.

"Nonstop information is being conveyed over the FEMA radio, and. It will continue to play until the sweep is complete in November."

Henry lifted his head in attention when he heard the shouting of Maria, his wife.

"Let us through now!" she screamed. "I am not a prisoner."

Henry stood as Maria burst into the Oval Office. She held tightly to their twelve year old daughter, Anna.

A soldier flew in behind. "Sir, I tried ..."

Henry held up his hand to stop him. "It's okay. Just wait there."

Maria moved toward Henry. "You son of a bitch. What the hell kind of executive decision did you just make?"

"Maria, I did what had to be done," Henry defended. "There is no way to protect the kids and the adults without separating them."

"Surrender? That is the term you used as you read off some paper. I know you did. I know you," she argued passionately. "Or I thought I did. This is wrong."

"What am I supposed to do? Let this country fall apart? Let it die?"

"Yes. Yes." Maria nodded. "Let the children stay with their parents."

"They're killing the parents who are only trying to help. Then what? Who will care for them?"

Maria shook her head. "They came in and just started packing a single bag for all of us. Then I heard what you said. You're a monster, Henry, for doing this?"

"Right now, yeah, I'm a monster. But I think as time moves on, I'll be viewed differently."

"As the President who performed genocide on the children?"

"Not all."

Maria closed her eyes tightly. "I am so upset. I don't want to go with you. I don't. How … how can you just pack up and leave while ordering parents to give up their children? How can you even begin to call yourself a good leader?"

"By leading by example."

Maria had her head buried to Anna and on those words, she suddenly looked up. "What?"

"I can't expect a parent to surrender their child if I don't surrender my own."

Maria's eyes widened. She looked down to Anna then to Henry who had nodded to the guard.

"No!"

"Daddy?" Anna sobbed out.

"No!" Maria fought the soldier who pulled for Anna.

Henry walked up to Anna. He laid his hand on her cheek and lowered his head to kiss her. "I'm sorry. I love you."

"Daddy, no!" Anna cried as the guard pulled her from Maria's grip. "Daddy, no!"

Henry turned his back, folding his arms tightly to his body. He listened in pain as his own daughter screamed and cried, her voice fading as they took her. He didn't hear anything else. Not even Maria. He didn't know if his wife stayed or left, fainted or screamed. He listened to nothing but his daughter. What he felt right then was what every parent would feel.

He was part of a country that fought together and lost together. He made a decision that would burden him the rest of his life but it was one he had to make.

Renewal City: Hope

July 30 – Year 10 P.D.

Those who didn't live within the Renewal Cities didn't know. The cities were self contained, powered, and informed. Leaving the cities was permitted to go to other Renewals, but it was advised not to go beyond the borders and into unmanned America.

He was a first settler in the Renewal City of Hope. He didn't have a choice. He just had nowhere else to go. Within days, he was given a home and a job, one he knew how to do and wanted to do. It was best that way to stay on top of all information.

The only thing he didn't know was how things were in the other Districts or rather specifics. They received number of deaths and infections, but not who it was.

He'd find out soon enough.

From the balcony of his thirtieth floor apartment, he peered out to the street. It had returned to a pre -infection normalcy, but no one that lost would ever be normal until they knew for sure.

That day was at hand.

He received notice that the walls to the Districts would be opening in three days. It had been four years since the last infected died. It took six days to clear all that remained. The infected that took over towns and cities. They were cleared and it was labeled the 'Six Day' war, man's final war against the infection that would not die.

Too many avoided the Detaining, too many got sick. The infection mutated again, causing the same symptoms in younger adults as it did in children. The infected ran rampant and a final straw had to be drawn.

He remembered watching the missiles sail across the sky.

Because of his job, he knew the announcements that safe government transport would be provided to the Districts when they opened on a first come, first serve basis.

He was first to sign up to go to District Five, located just outside of D.C. – ages nine through twelve at the time of Detaining.

His bag was packed and he was ready to go. It was a three day trip, one that could end in heartache as easily as it could end happily. But he had to go. He had to know. He had to.

PART FIVE: GAME OVER

Chapter Twenty

October 31

Mon City, PA

Nola would do what she had to do.

Beforehand, while she prepared to implement her decision, she thought back. A year ago on Halloween, her children dressed like characters from a movie and she barely recognized them. Now, one year later, she barely recognized them again. Ben and Carlie were ravaged by the infection. Their bodies were mere skeletons, skin pasty white with pockets of sores. No matter how hard Nola tried to feed them, care for them, it was in vain.

They grew worse.

So did Nola.

It was time.

She used the light and that rendered them catatonic. She wrapped them in the big shirts, secured their arms, and carried them from the bedroom, one at a time.

In order to get to the van, she had to pass Eddie.

He puckered his lips, his face streaked with sadness. "Can I kiss him?" he asked about Ben.

Nola nodded and carried Ben to him.

"Bye, little brother. I'll think of you every day. Thank you." Eddie kissed him. "Are we doing the right thing, Mom?"

"We're doing the only thing we can. My heart is breaking, Eddie." She hugged Ben. "They're suffering and who am I keeping them this way for? Me? You? I can't do this."

Eddie lowered his head.

Nola carried out Ben and she then got Carlie. Eddie said his goodbyes to his little sister. It pained Nola to even leave the house, but she had to. She had to do what was best for her children.

After placing Ben and Carlie in the car, she walked back in the house.

Eddie looked up.

"Food is in the kitchen. There's plenty. Ration the water."

"Are you going to be gone that long?" Eddie asked.

"I don't know how long this will take." She hesitated by the door then rushed to her oldest son. She hugged him tightly. "I love you. You have been my life's greatest gift. Know that. Please know that." She planted her lips firmly to his forehead and held them there. Nola sniffed hard and then wiped her cheek. She hurried back to the door and looked once more at Eddie. "Everything I have done, I have done for you kids. I always will and am now."

"Mom? What's going on?"

Nola shook her head, holding back from crying. She smiled, then stepped back, closing the door.

She all but ran to the van, only looking back on more time at the house before she left.

The Option Center was only down the street and there was a lot of activity there. Nola waited for at least ten minutes before getting out of the van. Ben and Carlie began to stir. A soldier helped her bring the kids inside.

Nola cried the entire time.

She held Carlie in her arms as she signed the final papers.

"I'm so sorry," the woman at the counter said. "I am very sorry. We'll take her now."

"No, I want to go back."

"Are you sure?"

"Yes. I'm going to be there. Is that allowed?"

The woman looked down to the clipboard. "Yes … Nola, it is." She walked from behind the counter. "Follow me."

Nola did. As they walked down the long hallway, she felt Carlie stir in her arms. She didn't have a fear of being bitten.

Carlie was always calm for an hour after being hit with the light. She expected calm. She didn't expect …

"Mommy?"

Nola's heart dropped.

"Mommy what's going on?" Carlie asked.

"It's okay, baby." Nola held her tighter. "We're gonna go play" She pulled Carlie from her so as to see her face.

"I'm scared. I'm sick, Mommy. I'm so sick."

"I know. It'll be better soon. I promise."

"Are you crying, Mommy?

"I am."

The woman opened the door. The room looked like a day care with a big glass window. The soldier was already untying Ben's arms and he placed Ben in a small chair by a table full of toys.

Nola carried in Carlie. The room had an odd ammonia smell to it. She placed Carlie in the chair and undid the restraints. She ran her hand down her daughter's face and kissed her.

"Are you leaving? Don't leave," Carlie cried. "Please, Mommy, don't leave."

Nola looked at Ben. He had been staring out and then suddenly, for the first time in weeks, not only did he make eye contact with Nola, he smiled.

Nola sobbed. She hurriedly hugged him, kissed him, and stood straight.

Her entire being shuddered and shook and then Nola looked to the woman.

"Please, Mommy. Don't leave me." Carlie cried.

"No worries, sweetie. I'm not." Nola sat down on the little chair between her children and pulled them both into her. She lifted her head and looked to the woman who stood at the window.

Nola nodded at her and smiled.

The door closed.

After her heart had dropped, Nola assured herself she was doing what was best for all the children. Eddie would realize that someday. She looked up when she heard the hissing. After passing another round of kisses to her children, she clutched them tighter and Nola took a deep breath. Her last deep breath of air.

Her last real breath of life.

Chapter Twenty-One

November 1

New York, NY

It didn't matter that Tom and Sam had told the children to be quiet. They cried anyway. They screamed and cried in fear at the banging of the church doors. So much so it caused the 'Sweep Patrol' to blast opened the locked church doors.

They stormed the church and the stairs that led to the basement.

They broke down that door with ease.

"There are no infected here!" Sam cried out as they broke through. "They're all healthy. Don't shoot!"

"Secure the children!" one of the soldiers yelled out.

There had been ninety-six children that Tom and Sam had cared for, protected, and came to know. It was over. Twenty soldiers entered the room and, in the middle of it all, Father Sam fell to his knees, broke down and cried.

He had been defeated.

Tom was not giving up.

During the commotion and confusion of gathering the reluctant children, Tom, clutching Jenny in his arms, made a run for it.

Her arms around his neck, legs to his waist, Tom mad a mad dash out the door, up the steps, through the vestibule, and out to the street.

He stopped cold when he heard the close sound of a weapon engaging.

Out front on the street were two gray school buses.

"Put down the child."

"No," Tom said.

"Sir, it is the law that the child must be detained."

"No. Just let us go. Just let us go."

Jenny cried, "Don't shoot my Daddy, please."

Tom held her tighter. "Listen, she's all I have. Please."

The young man, no older twenty-five, honestly looked sorry and compassionately to Tom. "I wish I could, . I can't. She has to be taken."

"Where? Where are they taking her?"

"The city is open now. You can leave. If you check in at a Renewal Center, they'll let you know. All I know is the Districts are separated by ages. I don't know where they are. They'll tell you but you got to hand her over. Please don't make me take her from you. Please, I've done that enough."

"Then don't do it now. Don't take my baby. Please, don't take her," Tom begged.

"If you make a run for it, if I don't take her, then what? The next guy will shoot you and take her? What good does that do her?"

Tom asked him for a moment. He didn't want to let Jenny go. He had no plans to do so. The young soldier afforded him the time while they loaded the other kids on the bus. Tom kept thinking, where he could run, what he could do, all the while telling his daughter he was trying. He didn't want to let her go. He would hold on until he couldn't.

Then Tom didn't have a choice.

When the last child was loaded, another soldier gave Tom one chance and then after an 'I'm sorry', he took Jenny.

Took her.

Tom screamed out, 'No!" and chased after, but he couldn't get through. He was held back until the door of the bus closed.

He couldn't breathe. He physically couldn't breathe and swore he was having a heart attack.

Trying to keep his wits, Tom saw her. Jenny barged through to a window and banged against the glass.

He heard her screaming his name while crying insidiously, "Daddy! Daddy!"

She kept crying and calling for help. Tom ran to the bus, reached up to the window, and then the bus pulled away.

He could still hear her crying even as the bus turned the bend. Maybe he wasn't really hearing her;. It could have been his imagination or just his heart playing that painful moment over and over. Whatever the case, he heard her and would always forever hear that scream.

Alone on the street, Tom folded. A complete emptiness consumed his soul.

He was done.

He lost his final battle.

Chapter Twenty-Two

November 2

Boardman, OH

"I'm sorry, I am." Opus lowered his head and stared down to his folded hands. His comment was out of context and had nothing to do with Ralph's discussion of figuring out how to keep the whole house warm during the winter.

Middle of that discussion, Opus said he was sorry.

"I can't do this." He stood. "I love you guys, I do. But I can't play wasteland survivor when civilization is on the other side of the country."

Bobby snapped. "What the hell? We are your family. We can't go. You know that. We need you."

"Bobby," Brady whispered as she cradled Sammy on her lap. "Stop!"

"No, I'm not gonna stop," Bobby said. "He wants to go."

"Let him," Brady said. "Let him. We can't ask this of him. We can't ask this of anyone."

Ralph shook his head. "You can ask family anything. We aren't gonna starve. We have an entire state at our disposal."

"And what will it be like?" Opus asked. "Next year or the? The year after? What? Savages, people fighting for scraps, killing? No, I can't do this. I'm sorry."

"Don't be," Brady said. "Don't. I don't blame you. In fact ….I want you to take Aunt Jean."

"What?" Aunt Jean barked. "I'm not leaving my home. No."

Brady stood and adjusted Sammy. "None of you should stay. Just me and Bobby. We can't expect this from you. Perseus, you go with your brother. Ralph …"

"Don't ask me." Ralph shook his head. "I'm not going. You're my kid, Brady. I'm not going anywhere."

Brady faced Howard. "Will you go?"

"Are you nuts?" Howard asked. "Leave Miss Jean? No, I'll stay. I chop wood pretty good."

Brady inched her way to Opus. "You leave in the morning and you don't look back and you don't feel guilty, you hear?" she said passionately. "I love you as much as I love anyone in this room. Sammy loves you. Maybe if you go, you'll be lucky enough to find out what's going on. We have the radio. We're gonna be in the dark."

"I'm sorry, Brady. I didn't want …" Opus stopped talking when there was a knock at the door.

"Hide the baby," Bobby said. "Go."

Howard snapped his finger and Brady handed Sammy to him. They waited until Howard was gone and Bobby walked to the door.

Cyrus stood there.

"Oh," Bobby exhaled loudly then called out. "It's okay, Howard. It's my brother. You can bring Sammy back." He then embraced Cyrus. "God, Cyrus. We were worried about you." He started to shut the door then noticed the Government Humvee. "You're not alone."

Cyrus shook his head. "I'm not here for a reunion, Bobby."

Bobby closed the door. "What's going on?"

"I … I am here for two reasons." Cyrus said. "I need Perseus. He's alive, well, and not sick. I need him."

Bobby nodded. "We were wondering about that. No problem."

"I'll go grab a bag," Perseus said. "Where are we going? To some lab?"

"You can say that," Cyrus answered, running his hand over his head. "It's gonna be a while before anyone sees you, Perseus. We're headed to a District."

"What!" Bobby blasted. "Perseus, do not leave! You are not getting locked in some prison camp for ten years!"

"Brother, it's the only way," Cyrus told him. "I need him to work on a cure, antiserum, antibacterial, anything. I need him."

Perseus held up his hand. "I'll do it. I want this thing to stop. It's cool. I mean, Bobby, we'll see each other again in the future."

"Actually ..." Cyrus cleared his throat. "All the time, Bobby...you've been recruited as a volunteer. I had to pull some strings. They were only taking men and women with military or medical background, but I told them you are a mechanical genius and ..."

"What the hell," Bobby laughed in ridicule. "I'm not volunteering. To do what? Go to a District with Perseus? Why would you even think I'd do that?"

Cyrus looked down then with a solemn face, made eye contact with each person in the room before he said. "So you could watch your daughter grow up."

Brady's entire being shook and her legs wobbled. "Oh my God."

Bobby looked at her, then to his brother. It was delayed, but finally Bobby understood what Cyrus was saying. "Are you fucking kidding me?"

"All children are to be surrendered."

Brady saw it coming, and she dove forward at Bobby, lunging at him before he struck Cyrus.

Then Ralph stepped in, being the only big enough to hold Bobby back.

"Let me go, Ralph. Let me kill my brother because he is not taking my kid."

Opus had a painful whine to his voice. "Cyrus, Why? Why would you do this? Why would you disclose where she is."

"Why? Because she has to live ..." Cyrus said with edge. "Sammy has to live and this is the only way I can make sure she does."

"Cyrus," Brady whimpered. "She's here. She's safe. She's away from everyone ..."

"She's more than likely infected," Cyrus said. "Eighty percent of all young children have it. It's doing nothing to them. It's dormant, but the moment they get old enough, it will hit. I have to beat it in them now –, right now, because we don't know if this thing will mutate and strike earlier. We just don't know."

Bobby barked. "So leave her here until you get the cure."

"Then what?" Cyrus asked. "Airmail it? Drop it? How do you propose I do that when I'm behind the walls of a District? They're serious, Bobby. Those walls won't open. I'm going in too. She'll be at the main research District."

"No." Bobby shook his head.

"I never liked you much, Cyrus," Ralph said. "You take that child, I'll shoot you. No questions asked. I will shoot you."

"Thank you for the warning." Cyrus then turned to Brady. "Please. Listen to me. If you don't hand her over, they will come in and take her."

Brady cradled Sammy tightly.

Cyrus lowered his voice. "Is that how you want the goodbye to be? Violent? Screaming? Her lasting memory of you is of all of you freaking out? No. She's leaves, Brady. She has to."

Brady closed her eyes tightly. She heard Sammy whimpering in her ear. "I can't give her up. I can't give up my baby."

"I'll be there. Bobby will be there. So will Perseus."

"I won't be. Why can't I be there?" Brady said. "I'll go. I'll … I'll volunteer."

"It doesn't work that way," Cyrus said softly. "I don't want to take her. I don't. But this was my only way to save her. You may miss years, but you'll get her back. She'll be alive."

"No," Bobby snapped. "No. Cyrus, leave this house, tell them she isn't here."

Brady's hand cradled Sammy's head and she sat down. "Bobby, go pack a bag. Perseus, you too."

"What?" Bobby stormed to her. "No."

Brady nodded. "I will not have her ripped from my arms. This is hard enough as it is. If she has to go, I will send her with my love and promises, but I will not have her ripped from me. She's already being ripped from my soul." She peered up, her eyes glossy. "Go, because I have to say goodbye to you too."

Brady pulled Sammy's arms and looked at her daughter. She shifted her eyes to Perseus. "Perse, Aunt Jean has that picture of us. Can you take that?"

"Yeah, Brady, I will." Perseus replied.

"Pap?" Brady sniffled and looked to Ralph. "Say goodbye. Okay?"

"This is insane, Brady." Ralph walked to Sammy and crouched down.

"Am I going bye-byes?" Sammy asked.

Ralph nodded. "Yeah, you're gonna go with Daddy and Uncle Perseus and Uncle Cyrus. I am going to miss you more than anything." Ralph palmed his hand against her cheek and then laid his lips to her. "I love you. I love you so much. Thank you for giving me meaning. I promise, when you are coming home, I will be right there waiting. I will be right there when you and Daddy come out."

"Mommy too?"

Brady answered her. "I'll be there whole time. You just …. You just close your eyes and think of me. You talk to me and I will feel you and hear you because I am here." She pointed to Sammy's chest. "And you are here." She laid her hand on her heart.

Ralph inhaled a sad sluggish breath, kissed Sammy again, and stood.

"Now you have to go before Mommy doesn't let you go." Brady stood and walked Sammy to Jean. "Say goodbye to Aunt Jean."

"Bye, Aunt Jean." Sammy leaned to her and kissed her.

"Goodbye, Little One. Lots of love. Be good." Aunt Jean puckered.

Opus reached to Brady and took Sammy in his arms, holding her for the longest time. He was emotional when he handed her back.

Howard leaned forward and kissed Sammy. "You be good. I'm gonna watch your Mom for you. Okay?"

Sammy nodded. "George. Can I take George?"

"The puppy." Brady peered at Cyrus. "Can she bring him?"

"Yeah." Cyrus answered.

Howard handed the wiggling dog to Sammy.

Sammy giggled. "I have George with me. It'll be okay. He's my friend. He's brave."

"Like you." Brady told her then she saw Bobby. Her heart broke again.

"Baby, I don't want to do this." Bobby stepped to her. "I don't."

'You have to be with her," Brady told him. "You watch our daughter. You watch her with your life and you tell her every night how much I love her."

"I will." Bobby's lips quivered and he wrapped his arms around Brady. His kissed her firmly on the lips then moved his mouth toward her ear. "I love you. Know that and remember that every night."

"I'll be right there waiting for you. I promise," Brady said and stepped from his hold. She tried to be brave. She thought of what Cyrus said. She wanted Sammy to see a loving mother not a screaming hysterical one. She wanted Sammy to feel love not fear and she transferred Sammy from her arms to Bobby's.

Perseus walked up and grabbed Brady, hugging her. "I have this. I'll be there. I'll make sure I do my part."

"I know you will." She kissed him then kissed Cyrus on the cheek. "Fix this. Get my daughter back to me."

"I will." Cyrus reached back and opened the door.

Bobby's eyes stayed on Brady the whole time. His face was red, his nostrils flaring, and his eyes glossy. He paused at the door and before he stepped out, Brady raced to him and with such intensity, she threw her arms around him and Sammy one more time.

They stayed that way and then she let go.

"Bye, Mommy. I love you."

"I love you, Baby." Brady lifted her chin and smiled for her daughter. She held that firm, strong, confident look until they walked out.

She couldn't watch them walk from the porch or get into the car. She couldn't.

The second the door closed, her walls of valor fell and Brady crumbled to the floor in heartbroken defeat. Body shaking, she sobbed uncontrollably. There was no comfort to be found.

The two people she loved most in life had just left and she didn't know when or even if she would see them again.

Chapter Twenty-Three

Mon City, PA

Staff Sergeant Haggard had seen it all. He could honestly say with the Tantrum infection there was nothing left that would surprise him.

He had been part of Operation Clean Sweep since its unofficial commencement a week earlier. Mainly he was a 'red flag' man, a spotter who walked in front of the slow moving truck, looking for red flags or wayward infected. On his helmet was a strobe light and he wore battle gear. Haggard was indeed facing battle.

His stretch of duty started with his reserve unit in Carlisle, PA located right outside of Harrisburg.

Ten days letter he was across the state. They finished Washington, PA and hit the string of small railroad towns, towns that had been abandoned by the younger population and children were the minority. The towns were mostly barren save a few roaming infected and a flag or two. They had made it down four blocks of Main Street without incident or seeing anything. Haggard peered slowly left to right and then saw the redness of it long before he got to the older house. It was a contrast to the old white home.

"Up ahead," Haggard hollered and lifted his arm in a signal then pointed to the house.

The trailing truck slowed down and two soldiers leapt from the back and trotted up to join Haggard.

Leading the way, Haggard walked up to the porch first. He instructed his team that firing was a last resort, to use gas first. He had lost two kids of his own to the infection and to him, the illness was bad enough. They didn't deserve to be gunned down like rabid animals.

He waited for the others to join him on the porch then gave the signal to raise their weapons. It would go as it always did. He'd have someone open the door and he'd go in first. It was dangerous but a part of Haggard didn't care if he lived or died.

The old home had a huge porch and a line of windows. Haggard walked the length of the porch and peered in the window.

"There's one. Dining room. Not moving. Stationary." He took a step, paused, and did a double take. "Fuck me. What the hell? This is a first," he said. "Lower your weapons."

Tom wallowed in his grief for only so long then he grabbed the first car he could see, siphoned gasoline for it, and drove. He wasn't sure he'd make it. He didn't take a huge car, but one that would be great on gas. He knew his destination.

It was an eleven hour trip that took only eight hours. No traffic, not police, no one. The world was a dead place and the longer Tom drove, the more he saw this.

He wasn't quite sure where Nola was staying. He had the address and since it was Main Street, he figured it would be easy to find. The last he spoke to his sister, she was in a similar situation. Her children were healthy and Tom could only guess they were taken in the Clean Sweep as well. His plan was simple, get Nola and Eddie and head to Dayton to try to get into a Renewal City. There'd he'd find out where Jenny was going and he'd wait it out. What choice did he have?

By the number on the houses and business Tom knew he was only a block away, but he had to pull over because two large military trucks blocked the street. He parked the car and stepped out.

He read the house numbers. Nola's address was an even number and Tom was on the even side. He immediately grew sick to his stomach when he saw his destination. The military was already there. The red flag hanging from the second floor window crushed him. He envisioned Nola trying to help her sick kids only to be attacked and killed. Poor Eddie, too helpless to even move, was a waiting target.

He turned his back, would take a moment, and then check on things but he had to get it together. He had travelled with hope only to face another heart ache.

"Uncle Tom!"

Tom heard the call of his name and spun.

Eddie.

Two soldiers were lifting his wheelchair and carrying him from the house.

"Uncle Tom, help!"

Yes. Yes, he would and yes, he could. Finally a situation where Tom could be in control. He rushed to the soldiers. "Stop! Stop! Where are you taking him?"

"A flag was hanging on the window," the soldier said. "He's a minor. We can't leave him."

"I'll take him. He's my nephew." Tom said. "I'm here now."

"Are you sure?" the soldier asked.

"He's sixteen. He's not infected. He's fine. He's exactly what I need right now." Tom smiled and the second they put down the chair, Tom embraced Eddie. "God, Eddie, you don't know how much I needed to see you." Tom kissed him.

"My mom took Ben and Carlie to the Option Center two days ago. She never came back," Eddie said. "I don't think she is."

"My name is Sergeant Haggard." He shook Tom's hand. "We think …The mom left the red flag so someone would find him. Food, water, and his clothes were all within his reach."

"I have him now," Tom said. "Thank you."

"Are you heading to a Renewal City?" Haggard asked.

Eddie jumped in with an answer. "We can't. The news said only able bodied. I'm not able bodied."

"Son, that's not true." Haggard stated. "You are able bodied. You just don't walk as well as the rest of us."

"Then that's where we'll go," Tom said.

Eddie looked up at Tom. "What about Jenny?"

Tom shook his head. "She was taken in the Sweep. She didn't die like her brother."

"We have a truck heading down to Wheeling," Haggard said. "Transport leaves from there to Dayton if you need a ride."

"Yes. We'd like that. Thank you."

"I'll send them for you." Haggard nodded and as he stepped away to leave, he paused. "I'm sorry for you loss. I lost two of my own in this."

"I'm sorry for your loss too, son." Tom told him.

Haggard nodded in acknowledgment then after a swing wave of his arm, he gathered his soldiers. He yelled back to Tom to wait on the porch. A truck would be there shortly.

Tom believed him.

"I'm sorry you're stuck with me, Uncle Tom."

"Oh my God, no." Tom crouched down to Eddie. "More than anything, Eddie, you just saved my life. You ..." Tom laid his lips to Eddie's head. "You just saved my life."

Tom left New York a desperate man. He felt he had nothing, that he had lost everything. But he didn't. He still had something left. He had Eddie. He found hope. And he would hold on to the both of them for as long as he could.

Chapter Twenty-Four

District 3

December 1

Bobby parted the blinds and watched as the snow fell. He was on the fortieth floor. He watched for a while. Not many buildings remained which made it easy to see the huge concrete wall they were building in the distance. A wall that would surround the city.

He was one of the lucky ones – special. He got special treatment and a whole floor to himself. Not many had that. But as a volunteer, he not only had mechanical duty, he had to constantly check the children.

"This is not going to work." Bobby turned from the window and faced Cyrus. "All you hear is children crying. Babies, Cyrus, there are babies here. There aren't enough people to hold them, love them. They'll be shells of humans."

"They'll be alive." Cyrus said.

"There's more to life than just being alive."

"Yeah, being alive and healthy," Cyrus said. "I'll have this beat, Bobby. Perseus and some others are a start. They are immune. I'll have this beat in under a year."

"Then we can go?" Bobby asked.

"No." Cyrus shook his head. "This District holds the highest stakes. This District holds every child still within a year of getting infected. Right now, we need to secure them and make sure they walk out through the walls alive."

"There are tens of thousands of children here, Cyrus, crammed into high-rises with very few adults. It's no way to live."

"Neither is being infected. If I succeed, none of these children will ever be infected. That's a whole lot of future preserved."

"At what cost?"

"At any cost."

Bobby didn't know whether or not the choices made were correct. Sammy cried nightly for her mother. He supposed in time that would stop. In time, all the children would eventually stop crying.

The Government, in a short time, had created a sterile world. A protected world and, soon enough, a sealed-in world.

It was one of five Districts.

Bobby wasn't certain how long the Districts would hold or if they even would work. He just knew he'd do everything he could to make sure he and his daughter both emerged from the District alive and well; emerging, emerged into a safe world that was free from the infection, free from worry.

In a sense they were isolated from everyone and everything.

Some called it the end of the world. It could easily be that but Bobby knew as long as one District survived, one District emerged with survivors then it wouldn't be the world's end. All the suffering, the sacrifices, the surrendering would be worth it.

That was what Bobby held on to. That … and his daughter Sammy.

TEN YEARS LATER

August 2

District 5 – Former Washington, DC

Tom arrived with about eighty others to the main walls of District 5. It wasn't what he expected. Everything was overgrown, the roadways leading there and the area around the wall. The Washington Monument was a vine haven, looking as if it were ready to crumble at the simplest of touches.

The bus ride was a long one coming from the Renewal City and he was glad he left Eddie behind. Eddie wouldn't have handled it, although the head strong young man said he could.

Besides, Tom didn't know what he would see. Jenny would be nineteen years old. Would he recognize her if she survived?

That was the question.

Statistics rolled in constantly for the first eight years and then they staggered. Power was diminished to every District and only focused on the walls that were charged electrically and wouldn't power down for ten years. Despite what they told everyone, the walls were set.

They knew when they took the children it was going to be ten years.

District 5 was ages nine through twelve. Each year more and more children succumbed to the virus. No names were ever given, because every child was given a number.

Year Two, a cure was found, but by then, over forty percent of the children in District 5 had died. The cure 'recipe' was shared between Districts and it was not known if it worked better in one than another. From what Tom learned, it wasn't really a cure, more of an inoculation or inhibitor that had to be constantly given to the children, like a yearly booster. It was generated from the very few who were immune all together to the infection.

Tom just checked the daily posts.

Now here he was waiting with others in front of the open wall. There was one person he recognized. Standing alone was Henry Collingsworth, the former President of the United States. His own daughter was behind those walls.

They waited.

Where were the occupants of District 5?

It took about an hour and then they started to trickle through. They weren't children. They were adults. Some emerged and looked around and then dropped their head in disappointment.

Each female that passed through Tom wondered if that was her? Was that Jenny? He begged in his mind that he'd recognize her.

With each person that walked out, he felt more disappointment. He looked at the President who was still searching for his own child, a child that never did come out.

Then Tom saw her. Jenny. She was looking at the faces and when she connected with Tom, she smiled widely. Arms extended, she pushed through the others and hurried to him, shrieking loudly.

She was frail and thin and as his arms wrapped tightly around her, he felt her bony frame. Immediately, Tom began to cry. He had waited for this moment for ten years.

Ten years of hoping. Praying. Waiting. Wanting. The pain never got easier but in that second, as he held his daughter, everything was better.

<><><><>

District 3

To Brady, it was nothing shy of the end of the world. A flattened city, surrounded by a concrete wall was embedded in a new jungle of foliage. Nuclear war had ravaged so much of the land, or at least that was what she heard.

Brady had never left that wall. For ten years she made her home just outside that wall and she waited.

After Cyrus informed them which District Sammy was being held, and where that District was, Brady chucked everything, bought a camper, bartered for all the gas she could, and travelled to that District.

She was one of the first to arrive and couldn't get through the tunnels that led to the city. When she finally got through the tunnels, when the military blockade lifted, she saw the wall. All the bridges had been destroyed.

Her child and husband were prisoners in a protective world.

Finding another way around the city was easy and though time consuming and gas consuming, she did it. She parked her camper and made her home, vowing to never leave and she didn't.

She had spoken to Ralph and Opus many times.

Ralph and Opus even took turns coming to the wall, visiting and bringing supplies. Howard even came and stayed a while but he then went to District 4 where he hoped his own children were taken.

But contact with all of them stopped.

When she learned of the Six Day War, she figured they had passed away.

Brady didn't know that for a while, a section of the United States was impassible.

She waited by that wall. Thousands had been there early on and they slowly left, giving up hope – but not Brady. How many times did she try to break in? That was early on when the place was still heavily guarded.

She lived a very lonely existence. Her focus was only on Bobby and Sammy.

Then the walls opened.

No electrical charges. Brady pushed open that wall. She had no clue or idea how far away everyone was or if anyone was alive.

She was certain she looked different, older and worn. She had buzzed off her hair on a regular basis. It was the only way she felt clean.

What once was a city was overgrown. Grass and weeds pushed through the concrete of the streets and sidewalks.

She walked slowly down the streets of District 3, she wanted to call out. In fact, she was ready to when she heard the barking.

A dog?

The dog barked loudly and viciously and then Brady saw him running toward her. She lifted the pipe she carried for protection and readied to swing at the beast when he raged at her. Then she saw it. The pink homemade collar. One that was too big ten years ago.

"George?" Brady tilted her head. "George?" She upped her voice.

Would he recognize her? Attack her?

The German Sheppard mix rushed to Brady, snarled, and then stopped.

"George?" Brady said happily. "It's me? Do you know me, fella?" She knelt down and George ran to her. His tail wagged and the beast of an animal happily nuzzled into her. "That's a good boy. Where's Sammy? Where is Sammy?" She asked as she petted him. If George was alive, well, and adjusted then Sammy and Bobby had to be.

"Hello!" she called out. "Hello! Anyone here! Hello!"

No answer. Just her echoing voice bouncing back at her.

As she knelt there, having her reunion with George, crying out for someone, she heard the call of her name. It came from behind her and not from the city.

At first her heart dropped then she slowly stood up and turned around.

Ralph, with a cane, was standing down the street.

Gasping out an 'Oh, God," Brady raced his way. She barreled into him. He was older and frail. "Ralph."

"I thought you were dead." Ralph held her. "I thought you were killed in the war. We were moved to a Renewal City."

"Opus?"

Ralph shook his head. "He never came. He was trying to make it back to you, to wait with you."

"How did you get here?"

"They were transporting people here from the Renewal Cities for when the gates opened. I saw that damn camper and knew," Ralph said. "I knew you were still alive when I saw that camper."

"When I could get through the walls, I did. But no one is here, Ralph," Brady cried. "I waited and waited and no one is here. I thought ..." She noticed Ralph's stare had moved beyond her. "What?" she asked and then turned around.

A huge crowd of people had formed in the street. Young people, some of them still children. In front of them all, standing by George, was Bobby. Next to him was Cyrus and Perseus. They were all there. They looked ... good.

She immediately ran from Ralph and to the crowd. Her eyes fixated on Bobby and, as she neared him, she saw they looked as stunned as Brady felt.

Half way to them, Bobby broke free and ran to her. He grabbed on to Brady and swept her up into his arms, swinging her around as he held her tightly.

George danced and barked round them, his huge paws hitting against them as they embraced.

"I knew it," Bobby said. "I knew that was you out there. I put a sign up on top of the USC building but I didn't know if you saw it," Bobby whispered in her ear. "Oh God, Brady. I knew that was you."

"I couldn't leave. I couldn't."

"Mom?" the timid voice called out.

Every bit of Brady froze and her arms dropped. She stepped back from Bobby.

Sammy was stood there looking just as scared of Brady as Brady was of her. The little girl of three had grown up so much. Her hair was shorter but she looked exactly the same.

Brady only hesitated briefly and then she grabbed onto her daughter. She cried as she held her.

Reunited at last with her family.

There was no plan on what to do next where to go. Brady didn't think of that. All she focused on was seeing her family again.

The ten year wait outside that wall, the suffering and struggle, was worth it for that one moment of being together.

The infection was over.

The threat was done. The world had changed so much.

Where they would go remained to be seen. They could stay in the District, go west to the Renewal Cities or find somewhere in the middle to settle.

It didn't matter.

Brady's wait was over. The struggles were over. It was a new beginning, a happy one and one that she'd embrace as tightly as she did her family. As long as they were together.

Humanity faced its obstacles and path to extinction but, like Brady, refused to give up.

Life indeed ... would go on.

**